FATES ALTERED

USA TODAY BESTSELLING AUTHOR

JULES BARNARD

D1091295

FRESH FICTION BOOKS

julesbarnard.com

BOOKS BY JULES BARNARD

HALVEN RISING SERIES

Fates Altered (Prequel)

Fates Divided (Book 1)

Fates Entwined (Book 2)

Fates Fulfilled (Book 3)

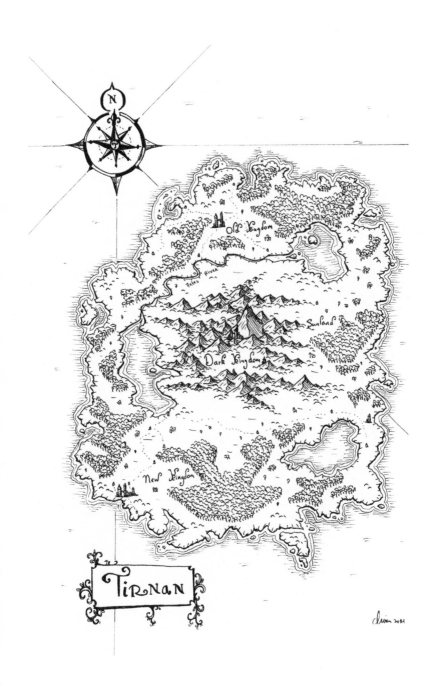

TIRNAN, THE FAE REALM, NEW KINGDOM CASTLE

"You will marry him."

Theodora Joelle Rainer stared blandly in the mirror of her vanity, her long blond hair hanging down her back in a smooth drape. She maintained a blank expression in the face of her father's bold statement, because Sihtric Rainer, leader of New Kingdom, saw fear as a sign of weakness. "Don't make me." Her voice didn't hitch or modulate, though her heart raced.

"There is nothing to be done," her father said, speaking to her from the doorway of her chamber. "Adelmar Lucent is the head of my guard and he has two brothers, Theodora. *Two.* Nearly twins at only fifty-eight years apart. Your mother and I were fortunate to have sired two children over five hundred years. How many Fae can lay claim to such a blessing as two children within a single century? His parents are still young and may yet have more children. His family's fertility coupled with their close ancestry to noble Fae makes him the best match."

It was an old argument, but she needed her father to see reason before it was too late. "I do not wish to marry him, or anyone. At least not yet. Most women my age have not married."

Theodora was chronologically just over a hundred years old—roughly twenty years by human standards—and barely into Fae adulthood.

The king took in a steadying breath, though his eyes pierced her with frustration. "Did you not hear of the beheading of the Oldlander king's child-bride?"

Yes, she'd heard.

The Oldlander king to the north was unpredictable and barbaric. A killer. When his young bride hadn't produced an heir the first annum of their union, he had her decapitated.

To expect conception that quickly among their kind was ridiculous, yet it was said the Oldlander king would choose a different female every annum until a child was born. He believed the lore of a son who would bring justice to his land. They said he would stop at nothing until it came true and Tirnan was under one rule—his.

For now, Old Kingdom was second in power to Theodora's land of New Kingdom. Theodora's father had no wish to overthrow their neighbor, but the same could not be said for the Oldlander king. He wanted it all.

"The only way to protect New Kingdom from this madman is to strengthen it with more Rainer blood, which means grandchildren. As many as possible. Only through our descendants will we grow more powerful."

All Fae possessed powers, but children with the richest angelic lineages possessed the strongest abilities, and her father's bloodline had some of the strongest in the realm. She understood his wish for the match with Adelmar; she just didn't like it. And she didn't want to sacrifice herself for an eventuality that might never occur.

Theodora's brother, who'd been married these last three hundred years, was still childless. She could end up childless too, and her sacrifice would be for nothing. And if it wasn't—if she bore a son or daughter to Adelmar—she had no wish for her child to be used as a weapon for her father's control.

The Oldlander king's erratic behavior made her father and his advisors nervous. When her father grew nervous, he made rash decisions. Theodora was presently on the receiving end of one such decision.

Panic rose inside her chest and she clenched her hands atop the vanity. She peered at her father in the looking glass.

Despite her every attempt to remain unmoved, he must have sensed something in her expression. His shoulders squared and his face grew taut, but she thought she detected uncertainty in his eyes. "I must leave for my meeting. Prepare yourself. The wedding will take place tomorrow." He spun and stormed past the door and down the hallway, the sound of his boots barely audible on the stone floors.

Light, efficient—Fae clothing was prepared for battle or whatever sacrifice was necessary for the betterment of the kingdom. Much like a noble Fae daughter. And it appeared it was Theodora's turn.

Adelmar. The man was certainly *addled.* Her father wouldn't be pleased if she accidentally-on-purpose strangled her new husband in his sleep. No, she must do something to stop the marriage. And she must do it now.

As long as she remained in Tirnan, she had no choice in whom she married. It wasn't safe for her to venture to another land within their realm. The ruler of Old Kingdom would just as soon have her imprisoned as provide her shelter. Or worse, marry her in order to gain power over Theodora's father. She didn't wish to lose her head if she failed to produce a child for the Oldlander king.

A bargaining chip—that was all she was to her father and the Oldlander king; even to Adelmar, who wanted more power within her father's land.

Sunland, the third kingdom in Tirnan, was an option for

escape. They were pacifists by nature. But she wouldn't be able to hide there forever. Her father would find her, and she'd be back where she started, committed for eternity to a man she didn't respect or love.

A light scraping came at the door.

"Enter," Theodora called.

Her companion Portia swept into the room carrying fresh nightclothes. "Would you like to change, my lady? You have a big day tomorrow."

Theodora angled away to hide her nervousness. "Not now, but thank you. Please leave them on the chair and close the door behind you." She hated to send Portia away so abruptly, but she needed to act while she still could.

Portia's eyelids fluttered in confusion, but the older woman bowed and left the room, closing the wooden door behind her with a sound *thunk*.

Theodora rushed to the door and engaged the latch to seal herself inside. She had one option left, and it was dangerous.

To avoid marrying Adelmar, she must leave the Fae realm.

She ran for the tall wardrobe, tearing off her court clothes along the way, and grabbed the farmer's garb secretly tucked at the back. She had purposely stashed the clothes in the filigree box that would normally hold jewelry, knowing her companions and servants would never touch palace treasures without permission. It had been an emergency maneuver on her part, with the hope she would never need to use it.

It seemed she was wrong.

Dressing quickly, she grabbed the dagger her father had given her when she'd first learned to fight, and then she slipped on the gold bracelet from her brother.

Theodora stood before her vanity and stared at her reflection. Her white-gold hair glowed in the dim candlelight...as it likely would in the dark.

This would not do.

She removed the gold circlet atop her head and set it gently on the vanity. She plaited her hair in a simple braid down her back.

Her mother would find the circlet and know something was wrong.

Theodora pressed her hand to her stomach and the knot that had formed there. She didn't want to leave her family—her mother, brother, or even her father, who had stubbornly ignored all her wishes these last several months.

Perhaps she would return one day. Perhaps her father would realize how poor a match Adelmar would have made and see that she had been right to leave. It was her only hope.

She tucked her braid into the warm cap that covered her ears, and a sparkle at the corner of her vanity caught her eye.

Theodora reached out and ran her index finger down the deep amethyst pendant dangling there, the facets of the diamonds that framed the stone catching the light. Though less valuable than her most simple court ensemble, the necklace was her prized possession. Her mother had given it to her on the eighteenth anniversary of her birth. It had been her grandmother's before that, passed down from one daughter to the next.

There was no place for such extravagance where she was headed.

She reached for the necklace anyway and fastened it around her neck, tucking it beneath the woolen tunic and cape she would use as a blanket when needed.

Bringing the necklace was a sentimental gesture, but one she clung to. Until her father saw reason, or Adelmar took his great virility elsewhere and married another, she had no choice but to leave the people she loved. With her sturdy clothes and small leather satchel of ground allon leaves, she could get by in nearly any land. The Earth realm, with its common people and lack of magic, was no exception.

Avoiding the guards that stood just outside her bedroom door, Theodora crept through two connected rooms into an antechamber with an exit that was rarely used. Taking a small pinch of powder from the magical allon leaves, she brought it near her mouth, spoke a message to the birds that pecked the castle grounds for food, and blew the powder into the air. She could speak to animals up close, but to send messages from afar, she needed the powder of the allon leaves to boost her ability.

She waited for thirty seconds, then peeked out the door of the antechamber.

The guards stared at a window at the end of the hallway, discussing the noisy birds that fluttered and danced in sweeping dips in front of the window—a window located in the opposite direction from where Theodora stood.

She quietly entered the hallway and hurried down the back stairwell used by servants. With the hood of her cape pulled low over her eyes and her head tucked down, she was unrecognizable but *very* circumspect. Only guards, servants, or high-ranking officials wandered inside the palace. The farmer's attire she wore would be useful on Earth and far more discreet than her court clothes, but it set her apart in the palace, and she needed to make it to the nearest portal without being recognized.

Theodora exited the stairwell to a wing rarely used except by soldiers, then jogged toward a secret egress known by few. Only guards used this access point, and if she ran into one of them, she would most certainly be questioned. But it was her best chance of escape.

She was nearly to the exit when male voices floated her way.

Her father's visit had ended at the perfect time. Between the changing of the guards and the servants busily preparing for the evening meal, she had hoped to avoid most, if not all, in this section of the palace. In the late afternoon, most officials were meeting with her father. Yet the distinct sound of male voices grew louder.

Theodora opened the closest door and slipped inside—and found herself in what could only be a guardroom. *Bollocks.*

She knew the grounds better than most palace inhabitants, but even she didn't know what hid behind every door. Particularly the ones that weren't used by the royal family.

Fortunately, no one was inside, though that could change if her suspicions about who approached were correct. She hadn't time to find another space in which to hide. Simple cots, a desk reserved for the highest-ranking guard, and a long table filled the room. And, of course, there were dozens of weapons secured behind metal bars.

She ran for the nearest cot and tucked beneath it, seconds before voices burst inside.

"Cannot believe you agreed to get leg-shackled," said one man.

"A small price to pay," came another voice, this time from someone Theodora recognized.

Adelmar.

If this was her luck today, she was doomed.

"I've secured my future. And have you not feasted your eyes upon the princess? What man would not want a beautiful virgin whose sole purpose is to provide him with children?"

The men chuckled, and Theodora rolled her eyes.

This was exactly why she despised Adelmar. Not only did he disparage her in front of his friends, but he cared only for himself. Worse, the man kissed like a water serpent. The one time he'd cornered her and snuck one in, she thought she might be sick.

Never again.

Blasted man. Not all Fae treated their women this way, but too often they did.

"She is said to be headstrong, Adelmar," the first guard said. "I'm going to enjoy watching her leash you."

Chuckles erupted around the room.

"There will be no leashing, you idiot," Adelmar's nasal voice rang out. "As you can imagine, I've made arrangements with my various *friends*. I will have ample female companionship while the princess is in our chambers tending to my every domestic need. The pleasures I've enjoyed won't cease just because I marry."

"And you think the princess will agree to this?" The bold guard let out a yelp, and the scent of burnt flesh filled the room. He must be a friend of Adelmar's, but not such a good friend that Theodora's intended wouldn't teach him a lesson.

Adelmar controlled fire and could scorch a man with precision, or engulf him in flames.

"She will say nothing once we are married. She may be a princess, but she will know her place—as do you."

Theodora clutched the small blade she'd brought with her and stifled the urge to poke him in the arse. Not even the brave guard commented this time, because Adelmar was vicious and, unfortunately, correct. Once married, she had no recourse. Her husband would have the backing of the kingdom where she and their future children were concerned. She could leave him after they married, but it would be infinitely more difficult, and she would lose whatever rights she had to any children they produced.

The men proceeded to discuss their female conquests over the last few days—Adelmar's list being the longest—while Theodora ground her molars and waited. Finally, they left the room.

Theodora wasted no time. She slipped into the hallway and ran out through the secret palace exit, calling to more animal friends.

Adlets were always up for a good herding—or attack. They were partial to both. Though they looked something like an Earth pig from the books she's read, adlets were more like a sheepdog by nature, drawing their prey through tactical distraction.

In this case, the adlets herded the numerous guards who circled the palace grounds away from the west gate, where the portal to Earth lay. They tripped the soldiers and caused a general ruckus without harming anyone.

With the guards distracted, Theodora could see the portal clearly now. There was no marker, only a wavering space in the air that, if you didn't know better, could be easily missed. But Theodora did know better.

She glanced back at the palace, her heart racing. This was the right thing to do; she felt it in her bones. Breathing in the scent of her homeland one last time, she ran forward and leapt through the portal.

To safety.

To a new life.

Theodora tumbled through light and color, keeping her eyes tightly shut, until she felt the pull of gravity. She arched her back and stretched her legs, landing on the other side of the portal and onto the land that housed Dawson University—the school Fae had built centuries ago in the human realm.

Her people used a human college campus to keep track of Halven, the unfortunate half-human, half-Fae children they produced. If her family hadn't already figured out that she'd left the palace, they soon would. And if Fae living on the campus discovered her, her father would be notified and she'd be sent home.

She couldn't return home. Not until the threat of this marriage was past.

Fleeing the campus, she kept to side roads that led south. She could have gone north, but she chose south for good luck, since her kingdom resided on the southern portion of Tirnan.

It was nighttime, thankfully, and she ran parallel to a main road, crossing farm and agricultural land. Her studies of Earth had taught her this was Central California. The land here was rural and less populated—more bovine than human—which she preferred.

Animals she understood.

Humans, with their lack of magic and short history, she understood not at all.

Over the next couple of days, Theodora spent her nights running in search of a place to hide. She never traveled during the day for fear of being seen by her father's men, who were surely looking for her by now. She appeared human, but she was tall, like all Fae, and couldn't be certain her presence wouldn't attract human attention and lead back to her people. For that reason, she took care to limit contact with others, eating the allon leaves she'd brought for temporary nourishment.

As she huddled inside the rough, single-room outbuilding she'd found on a large plot of land during the early morning hours of her third night on the run, Theodora's chest felt heavy. She'd crossed a good distance. At least a hundred and fifty miles separated her from the Dawson University stronghold where her people resided. No human could travel from the university to the middle of California's farmland on foot this quickly, but Fae were stronger, faster. In her realm, running was often the preferred form of travel. And if she could make that distance, so could her brethren on Earth.

This morning, she'd slept a few hours, then spent the late afternoon attempting to come up with a plan for how to survive on Earth without being discovered by her kind or humans. She'd made little progress.

The decision to leave Tirnan might prove disastrous. In her haste to escape, she'd thought only of the distance Earth would provide between her and her bridegroom. Among the greedy, shortsighted humans, she feared she might suffer a fate worse than marriage to a man she didn't love.

Humans were weaker, but if enough of them attacked, Theodora wouldn't be able to overcome them. What would happen if she betrayed her forefathers and accidentally revealed her kind existed, simply because of her presence in this land? Some humans knew, but they'd either been glamoured into forgetting, or they had reasons not to make it known. Unfortunately, Theodora's gift wasn't glamoury.

She glanced down at the gold band on her wrist. It wasn't a gift, exactly. She'd bartered for it with her brother, Beortric, in exchange for precious herbs that were difficult to obtain in New Kingdom. The bracelet helped hide her magic and, therefore, her presence from those of her kind. It had been a fair exchange. The herbs Beortric had wanted would have taken him days, possibly weeks, to obtain without the help of Theodora's animal friends. She'd delivered them to her brother in a matter of hours, with only a minimal amount of canine drool.

Beortric often had his head bent over some lab experiment, but she could count on him to help her. He'd married for love, and though he never said so, she suspected he knew she wished to do the same. Quite possibly, he even understood why she'd wanted the bracelet, which made her love him even more. He'd given it knowing her intentions.

She still needed to be careful—the bracelet wasn't foolproof. But if she hid from Fae and human alike, what then? Would she forever be alone? Even more distressing, she couldn't shake the feeling that despite the bracelet, her father would find her. He was a powerful man and she'd taken a great risk in disobeying him.

Theodora stared out the small window of the room she'd slept in, filled with tools secured to the walls and on top of shelves. The framed edges of the window were roughened, as though someone had cut it out as an afterthought. She watched the sky darken, her worries growing with the setting of the sun. Soon she would leave her hiding spot and once again search the land for some way to survive in this strange place. Perhaps she would travel toward the mountains in the east—

The sound of voices drifted in the evening air.

Male voices.

Theodora's heart raced. Fae realm or Earth realm, why must men traipse through her hiding places?

She rose abruptly from the rough wooden floor, her body tensing. If these men chose to enter the room, they would see her. There was no place to hide. Only the one door provided egress, and the small window wasn't wide enough for a child to get through, let alone a grown woman the height of a human man.

She considered the thick cloth folded in the corner. She'd used the cloth in the early morning for warmth, and it had barely covered her shoulders. Even if she curled into a ball beneath it, the floors were nearly bare. She would simply look like a tall woman hiding under a tarp.

The door jerked open and one of the men stepped over the threshold, holding a metal box in his hand and looking over his shoulder. "Tony, you need to chill. I'm not going out. I'm tired and I've got too much work tomorrow."

Theodora grasped the leather satchel at her waist, her other palm covering the dagger tucked in a hidden pocket at her breast, preparing for...she wasn't certain. In her land, she could very well be facing a battle. Trespassers in their kingdom weren't tolerated. But humans were different. She wouldn't use her magic unless absolutely necessary. She stood there, attempting to calm her breathing.

"You're like a eunuch, man," came the other male voice from outside. "Get out and have a fun."

"Why the hell do *you* want to go out? You've got a new baby and Leti at home. Leti will string you up by the balls if she finds you trying to get some."

These men had a different accent than the English spoken in her land, but the intent was clear. It was as if she'd stepped out of her hiding place in the guardroom of the palace and into a different lion's den.

Did all men have nothing better to do than talk about female conquests?

"Jackass, it's not me I'm thinking about. Of course I'd never cheat on Leti. I'm offering to be your wingman so that you can hook up. What do you say?"

The man before her huffed out a breath and his head turned slightly. And then, as if he sensed someone there, his gaze snapped to her, his body going very still.

After a second, his shoulders relaxed. He took in her face, the cap she wore on her head, then all the way down to her boots.

A shorter man stepped in the shed, pushing the other man aside. "What's up? Cat got your tongue, or are you finally relenting? Please tell me you relent, because you need to get laid—" His voice cut off as he took in Theodora across the room.

He looked quizzically at his silent friend, and his mouth twisted into a wry grin. "Don't want to go out, huh? You sly dog, you've been holding out on me."

Both men blocked the exit. There was no escape.

How odd that she could break out of a fortified Fae palace, yet be trapped in a human shelter smaller than a closet. In her defense, Fae protected against entrance, *not* exit. Even so, how was she to get away without revealing her magic?

Her choices were to attack with her dagger or let them make the first move.

———

SNAPPING out of his shock at the sight of the beautiful stranger in his shed, Alex hit his brother in the chest with the back of his hand. "Shut it, Tony."

He carefully set the toolbox he'd been carrying on the ground, never taking his eyes off the woman. The way her gaze darted to the side, she looked like an animal ready to spring at any moment. He couldn't look away.

Her face was perfect—pale skin, high cheekbones, rosy, plump lips. Only the fire behind her moss-green eyes implied a hidden strength to the gentle beauty. She was tall and willowy like a supermodel... Why was a supermodel hiding in his shed?

"Who is she, man?" Tony stage-whispered.

Alex shoved his brother back out. "Go home. I'll call you later."

"But—"

"Just do it," he growled.

She looked scared, and Alex felt the urge to protect her. He was almost six feet in height, but this woman had a good inch on him, though she was only half his width—all the Rosales men had broad shoulders. Regardless of her height, Alex didn't need his jackass of a brother frightening her any more than he suspected she already was.

"Fine," his brother said. "But you better call or I'll sic Leti on you. You know how she likes to gossip. And don't think I'm not telling her who I saw hiding in your tool shed."

His brother grumbled about stashing hot women and some other nonsense that was lost on Alex. Because there was something entirely unusual about the girl's eyes. The color was beautiful, but they were so clear that they appeared bottomless. And the intent behind them took Alex off guard.

Women in his hometown never saw the real man. They flirted, they leered, but they never saw the person he was on the inside. This woman barely checked him out, so intent was she on his gaze and any movements he made. It was as though his family's reputation meant nothing to her.

Alex's father ran Old Bob's land—the most profitable farm in the Central Valley. His father had built a nice living over the last thirty years, and Tony and Alex had taken up the business too, along with the notoriety that position meant in these parts. Alex and his family weren't rich by any means, but other than Old Bob, no one around here was. Still, men respected the Rosaleses, and women wanted a piece of the stability he and his brother could afford. Not to mention, women seemed to like the way they looked.

At twenty-four, Alex was tired of shallow intentions. He wanted someone to see the man, not the attractive breadwinner. He wouldn't mind having a wife someday. *Someday.* After he'd secured his family's future and fully taken over management of the farm from his father. More importantly, he wanted to find a woman who cared about the person he was and not simply the money and security he could provide. That was why this girl's genuine gaze stunned him. Off his jaded ass.

There was no hint she knew of him or cared one bit what he looked like. In fact, she stared at him like he was a nasty insect that had crawled into the shed.

"I'm Alex," he said, trying to break the silence and ease her mind. She'd pulled out a nasty-looking knife, and he got the impression she intended to use it. On him. "What's your name?"

She parted her full lips of the prettiest pale rose, but no sound came out, as if she hadn't spoken in a good long while and found the effort a challenge.

What had happened to her?

With her hair tucked up in some kind of wool cap, the delicate features of her face and blond eyebrows appeared ethereal. Her layered clothes draped in a strange and foreign way, but she didn't look as haggard as he'd expect if she were homeless. And she didn't look injured.

"Theodora. My name is Theodora," she said.

A frisson of awareness ran down Alex's spine. Her voice was more beautiful than her face, and that was saying something. She had an accent he couldn't place—British, but not.

"Theodora, are you okay? I mean, you're not hurt or anything, are you?"

Her shoulders straightened and she seemed to loosen her hold on the knife. "I am healthy."

He rubbed his forehead. "Good, that's good." Then he peered

around the space where he kept his tools on shelves and pegged to the walls. He spotted the folded drop cloth in the corner, which was a damn sight more orderly than when he'd tossed it there yesterday. "Let me ask you something, and don't take this the wrong way, but...did you sleep here last night?"

He studied her calm expression that conflicted with the tension of her other hand still clasped around a small pouch at her waist.

She nodded slowly.

"Okay." *Shit.* "Well, you can't stay here." She sucked in a sharp breath, and he held out his hand to stay her. "No, I mean, this is no place for you to sleep. The valley gets cold at night. You'll freeze to death." An exaggeration, but he couldn't stand the idea of her sleeping in a shed. He assumed she was in some sort of trouble if she'd needed to in the first place. And if she carried a knife.

"If you don't mind my staying another night," she said, "I don't mind the cold. My clothes are warm."

She didn't use puppy-dog eyes to manipulate him, yet her honesty was ten times more powerful.

"Theodora—" He stopped and thought twice about pleading with her. She didn't know him, and she didn't appear to trust him. Not with that knife still out, or the strange pouch she clung to like it was a weapon. He couldn't fault her for protecting herself. But he needed her to trust him if he was going to help her. He changed tactics. "My name's Alexander, but everyone calls me Alex. Does everyone call you Theodora?"

Her gaze darted to the side, as if she didn't understand the question. Then recognition shone in her eyes. "My brother calls me Theda—when he wishes me to do something for him."

Alex bit back a grin. Wherever her family was from, the sibling dynamics at least were the same as around here.

She couldn't stay another night in the shed for various reasons. That his boss wouldn't allow it and because it wasn't safe were the biggest concerns. And he knew of only one place close where he could keep her safe and figure out what had happened to her and how to help.

"Well, Theda, I'd like to ask you to do something too, but only because I'm concerned for your safety out here. What do you think about coming to my place?" He rubbed his forehead again and continued quickly. "I wouldn't normally recommend going home with a strange man, but I'm a good guy. Promise." He crossed his fingers over his heart, and her brow furrowed in confusion.

"The thing is," he continued, "I'd feel terrible knowing you were out here all night in the cold. I'd have to camp outside the shed to make sure you were okay, and then *I'd* be cold. So really, you'd be doing me a favor. My father, and my brother and his wife, live in houses right next door—"

"Yes." She squeezed the pouch at her waist again. "I will go with you."

A man she didn't know suggested she stay with him, and she leapt with both feet. Had she lost her mind?

The fears Theda had lived with over the last few days—of being alone for the rest of her life or worse, caught by her people —were to blame. Alex's offer seemed like the perfect way to become a part of this new world without drawing too much attention. And somehow, she trusted him.

Imperious and *arrogant* summed up most male Fae, but Alex didn't seem like the men she knew, which was a surprise, given the negative way her people referred to humans.

The conversation she'd overheard between Alex and the other man had helped her decide on whether to trust him. He hadn't been interested in hunting down women, and her instincts told her he was a good man, just as he'd claimed. Oh, she didn't trust him completely, and she hadn't lifted her hand off the magical allon at her waist, but she believed he meant to keep her safe for the night.

"It's getting late. Better follow me," he said, and stepped out of the shack.

Alex waited while she exited the small storage room, and then he circled back to the shed.

Theda edged quickly to the side.

He glanced at her skittish movements, but didn't remark on them. He pulled out keys and locked the small room she'd slept in. It hadn't been locked the night before, and perhaps he was correcting his mistake.

In her realm, Fae men would assume a woman was his for the taking after finding her in his quarters. But Alex appeared concerned, not controlling or calculating. He'd seemed uncomfortable asking her to return with him for the night, which was another reason she'd accepted. His concern for her welfare appeared sincere.

It had been a long time since Theodora's wishes were taken into consideration. It surprised her that the human male had.

Alex made his way to a green vehicle—squat with large tires, and covered in mud with a large crack across the front glass. She'd seen cars while traveling these last few days in the Earth realm, and now it appeared she was about to ride in one.

Fae powers weren't only genetic, they were strongest around the energy of other Fae, as well as Fae land. Cars polluted. To disrupt the unity of the land could be disastrous. Which was why there were none in Tirnan.

Alex opened one of the doors and eyed her. When Theda didn't move right away, he walked around the front of the vehicle and took a seat behind the wheel that made the car turn. "You still coming?" he called.

She walked toward the open door and lowered herself to the seat.

He seemed to be waiting for something else. When she peered over, he reached across her chest and closed the door next to her.

Right. Close the door, Theda.

She shook her head, her heart hammering at the warmth from

his arm where it had crossed her body. This man smelled good, like crisp forest air.

He started the motor and rolled down a dirt road. The sun had nearly set, looking like an orange sliver above the hazy, dark valley floor. Alex drove over a rut, and Theda braced her hands on the front console.

He peered at her from the corner of his eye, a smile on his face. "You okay there?"

"Yes, why do you ask?" She stared straight ahead, watching for any more body-rattling dips in the road.

"Well, you're holding on pretty tight, and I'm driving five miles an hour. You *have* been in a car before, right?" His chuckle died when she didn't answer right away.

"No," she finally said. There were some things she couldn't hide, and maybe if he thought her from someplace obscure, these things wouldn't seem out of the ordinary. "The town I'm from is —provincial."

Alex's jaw seemed to firm as he peered ahead. "Theda, are people looking for you?"

She turned to him, her first panicked thought—that he knew her secrets.

But he couldn't know of her defection. Still, his interest concerned her.

"You're not wanted by the police or anything, are you?" he asked.

She let out a sigh. *This* she could answer. "No, I'm not in trouble with the law." She hesitated, then said, "I've left my home. I wasn't—happy there."

"Okay." He nodded as if satisfied with her explanation, though he continued to glance at her with worry in his eyes. "Do you have friends? Someone we can call? The brother you mentioned, maybe?"

She stared straight ahead, her heart sinking. "There is no one."

Alex didn't know how he felt about Theda agreeing to stay the night with him. Sure, women had come home with him before, no questions asked, but they were from his hometown or the town over. Everyone knew everyone around here. This was different. Theda didn't know him from Adam. She could have asked to see his driver's license or to be introduced to his father, but she hadn't. She'd agreed without question.

He pulled up to his two-bedroom ranch-style house. He and Tony had painted the place just last year, so it was in decent shape. The furniture was a bit outdated, but he kept it clean—and why was he thinking of these things when he'd never cared what a woman thought of his place before?

He pulled the keys from the ignition and exited the Jeep, waiting for Theda to do the same. He closed the car door behind her and headed to the stoop, unlocking the front door of his house. "You hungry?" he asked as he walked inside.

Theda removed her hat, her blond hair tumbling down her back in a thick braid.

Alex nearly tripped over his own two feet. He swallowed hard. Blonde, she was just a blonde—nothing out of the ordinary. But her pale beauty mixed with that steely strength he'd glimpsed had an odd effect on him.

He shook it off. She didn't need some guy ogling her; she needed a warm, safe place to stay for the night.

She peered down, and her lips pressed together before softening back into a pretty heart shape. "I am a bit hungry."

He'd found her in a shed. Who knew when she'd last eaten? And Alex had the instinctive urge to feed and protect her—this person he didn't know. Which bothered him.

He'd always been good to women, even the ones he wasn't interested in. But he'd never felt a reflexive need to care for someone who wasn't his family.

22

Theda was unusually pretty, but there were plenty of attractive women around, and he'd dated many of them. Theda was fair, which wasn't as common in these parts, but that wasn't it either, because Alex had never preferred blondes to brunettes. He liked a pretty face as much as the next guy, but what had always kept him coming back for more was humor, kindness, and warmth—which he hadn't yet found in one person. It was also why he had never dated anyone long-term. And why he'd never experienced instant attraction.

The things he admired you couldn't see. They ran beneath the surface.

But with Theda, a woman he'd just met, he found his heart jumping around, pumping faster with every little flicker of her eyes or subtle movement of her hands. It was bugging the crap out of him.

He jerked off his work jacket and threw it on a hook by the door. He was helping a woman in need. Nothing out of the ordinary about that. He had to get out of his own head.

"Have a seat at the table and I'll make you something." He toed off his work boots and made his way to the fridge, pulling out bread and other ingredients.

She walked over and sat tentatively at the table.

"Turkey okay?" he asked.

Her eyes widened, then she nodded. God, he hoped she wasn't a vegetarian. The Rosaleses were big meat eaters. He had no idea how to prepare vegetarian food, but he could certainly buy her whatever ingredients she needed to fix her own. Something to worry about later.

He poured her a glass of milk and set it in front of her.

"Thank you," she said, tracking his movements, sending heat wherever her gaze touched his body. She seemed pretty fascinated by a guy making her a sandwich.

What jerks hadn't made her food before?

Not his problem. He shouldn't be worrying about how other

men had treated her...though if she'd been mistreated, that was something to consider. How would he get her help if he didn't know why she was hiding in his shed? He needed to figure that out first.

"So, Theda," he said, slathering mayo and mustard on a slice of bread and loading it with turkey, cheese, and lettuce. "You said there's no one you can go to, but you didn't say why you left. I don't want to intrude, but I think you should tell me what happened. I might be able to get you help."

Theda shifted in her seat, her gaze dropping to her lap. "I would rather not talk about it."

Alex paused, the butter knife suspended in his hand. "Was it that bad?" She didn't look beaten, but abuse could be hidden...

She must have heard something in his voice, because she looked up. "I was not physically hurt, if that is what you are asking."

He studied her face for a moment and decided she was telling him the truth. He continued making her a sandwich, and prepared one for himself as well. Not much of a dinner, but he was starved, and too tired to make anything more elaborate. "If it wasn't physical abuse, then did someone threaten you?" He placed the sandwich and plate in front of her.

She smiled her thanks and thumbed the napkin he'd given her. Her mouth turned down as she took a moment to respond. "They —wanted to control my life. In a way I did not wish."

Alex stretched his neck, tension building behind his shoulder blades. "Was it a guy? Was he trying to force you to..."

Her brow puckered. "No, not like that. It is difficult to explain. My family wanted me to do something that would cage me. Something that would have taken away my freedom, such as it was. If I hadn't left, their wishes would have been forced on me."

Alex sat in the chair next to her and bit into his sandwich, chewing woodenly as he considered her words. Was she from one of those religious groups where they made young women marry older men and work from sunup to sundown? Jesus, he'd read too many of Leti's—*secretly Tony's*—rag magazines. This wasn't daytime television. At least, he hoped not.

Theda didn't seem to be in imminent danger, but he didn't like what she'd told him, or the tension around her pretty mouth. That mouth told a story all of its own. Pretty, resolute, and infinitely kissable.

Kissable? Dammit, what was his problem? She was his guest, not a one-night stand.

Theda took a delicate bite of her food. She was being vague. Intentionally so. She didn't want to talk about where she'd come from, that much was clear, but eventually she would need to tell him. At least she'd shared some of her ordeal. Enough for Alex to know that she felt she'd had no choice except to leave.

"You're welcome to stay as long as you like." What was he saying? Her past could bring him all sorts of trouble. And he had no right offering her a place to live. He didn't own this home; his boss did.

Alex rented his place below market value from Old Bob. The same was true of Tony and his wife, and Alex's father. They all lived on the land for low rent in exchange for running the farm. They made a decent living on top of that, but Old Bob liked having them on site in case of an emergency.

Old Bob was a nosy old goat, though. He'd have something to say if he discovered Alex had moved someone in without checking with him first. Which meant his boss couldn't find out about Theda until Alex had a chance to talk to him.

"Maybe stay close to the house on this part of the farm. You know, for your safety." *And so Old Bob doesn't see you.*

He must be tired; he wasn't himself—harboring runaways who could get him in trouble.

Theda brightened. "Yes, that would be best. It is most kind of you to allow me to stay. And to prepare food for me." She studied his face as though she'd never seen anyone like him.

If she were any other woman, he'd think she was coming on to him. But Theda looked at him with true admiration, not as a means to seduce.

This woman was dangerous to his low-key existence. The quicker he got her help, the faster things could return to normal.

He finished off the last bite of his sandwich and stood, turning his back to her. "No problem."

And it wouldn't be. Alex would talk to Old Bob about Theda tomorrow morning. Then he'd figure out a way to help her and move her safely on her way.

4

Theda folded the soft white shirt Alex had lent her last night to sleep in, and placed it on top of the dresser. He'd even given her his bedroom for the night and slept on the couch because the other room in the house contained only a desk and chair. Alex had no notion of her roots, yet he'd been a complete gentleman, treating her like a princess more than her own fiancé ever had.

In her land, men did not cater to women; women catered to men. But Alex had prepared a meal just as a servant might. Perhaps these humans were different from the ones her people had studied? Or maybe humans had simply been observed through the eyes of male Fae who hadn't noticed such kindnesses?

Fae were not normally abusive to women, but neither was a woman viewed as an equal. A woman who wasn't clever never rose above the role of breeder unless she possessed strong magical powers. But even then, she was still used for procreation to ensure her powers lived on. Women weren't allowed to lead soldiers, and very few became advisors. This was changing, but a long history meant a long memory of how things had always been done. Millennia-long habits were difficult to extinguish.

Theda was a part of the royal family and allowed privileges

because of it, but she didn't possess aggressive powers. She wasn't much more than a breeder. But maybe in this land—where a man like Alex had found no shame in catering to her—Theda could become more than she'd ever hoped in her realm. She could build a life for herself on her own terms and earn the respect of both women and men.

It was more than she'd imagined possible when she'd entered the portal and left her home. For the first time since she'd arrived, a small smile pulled at the corners of her mouth.

She slipped outside Alex's bedroom to the water closet he called a *bathroom*. Though she trusted Alex thus far, she was too nervous to use the shower. Instead, she removed her clothes and sponged off, then put her clothes back on and cleaned her teeth with the new toothbrush Alex had given her.

She took a deep breath and re-entered the hallway, taking in the sketches along the walls. They were of the landscape she'd run past as she made her way to this property—farm and animals and sunsets—all beautifully rendered. Somehow the emotion pouring off these images gave her hope. Hope for a better future. Though she still had to figure out how to survive in this world. She couldn't live with Alex forever.

Sadness filled her at the thought. Which was silly. Of course she couldn't live with Alex forever. But he was kind, and she would miss it.

The smell of cooking meat and bread filled the room as she entered the kitchen and silently sat at the table. A plate and fork, as well as a glass filled with something orange, had been set out. Alex stood with his back to her, wearing thick blue pants like the ones he'd worn last night and a clean, fitted white shirt that stopped just above the large muscles on his tanned arms. She stared at his trim waist and the muscles in his back moving beneath his shirt as he worked over the stove, then glanced away, mentally scolding herself.

No wonder Fae had been tempted throughout history to make

love to humans, siring the half-bloods known as Halven. She found herself more tempted by Alex's physical appearance than she'd ever been by the Fae men she'd known. But then, Fae men had always treated her as a possession, while Alex had treated her like a person. Now that she no longer feared for her life, she was able to notice how handsome he was. But not so handsome that she'd risk more than friendship.

When born, Halven were the most unfortunate creatures, kept on Earth and never allowed in the Fae realm. They weren't tolerated by her kind, and neither were the Fae who produced them. Unless it was a male Fae who sired the child—then her people overlooked his indiscretions.

Over the years, a few males of noble blood had created Halven without punishment, though the children were never formally recognized. In fact, she'd known of at least one instance where the child had been slaughtered like an animal.

Barbaric.

Theda had never agreed with this treatment of Halven. Perhaps it was her connection with animals and the common spirit she saw in all living things. Killing wasn't something she wished to do in her long lifetime.

Alex began to hum, his deep voice sending a rush of heat down her chest. The tone of his voice, the way his body moved around the kitchen, his kindness—all of it had a powerful effect on her.

She shook her head. He'd offered his home, and she couldn't stop staring. Maybe she was more ready for marriage than she'd thought. Perhaps her father would let her return and marry a man of her choosing? Only that was the problem. Her father wouldn't budge on whom she married. To marry was to doom herself.

"Good morning," she said, to let him know she was there.

Alex turned quickly. "Sorry, I didn't hear you slip in."

"Did you create the drawings along the walls?"

He glanced down the hallway. "Those are old. I don't sketch much anymore. How did you sleep?"

"Better than in the small room."

A vee formed between his dark eyebrows. "You mean my tool shed? Yeah, I would think you'd be happier in a bed." He shook his head, looking unhappy. "No more sleeping in sheds, Theda. You'll stay here until you get back on your feet. Agreed?"

It was a kind offer she couldn't afford to pass up. Alex's home on the large farm was isolated, and the perfect place to hide out while she determined her next move. "Agreed."

"Good. How about some bacon and eggs?"

She had no idea what bacon was, but eggs she loved. "That sounds wonderful."

Alex carried over a pan and scooped scrambled eggs onto her plate. He set it back on the stove and grabbed a dish with strips of meat above thin paper, the grease soaking through. He forked two strips onto her plate and dished out some for himself. He glanced around the counter and picked up a platter with a cover on top. He set it in the middle of the table. "Toast."

The scent of warm bread and grease filled her nose, making her stomach rumble. She'd eaten very little these last few days, aside from the sandwich Alex had made her last night. And though Fae could survive much longer than humans without food, she was eager to eat more.

Theda waited for him to finish putting dishes in the sink before she touched the food, but her belly rumbled again.

He sat, scanning her. "Dig in. You don't need to wait for me." He scooped a large forkful of eggs and shoved it in his mouth. Once he swallowed, he bit off a piece of the meat and chewed, watching her.

Theda took a small bite of the strange meat, and decided it tasted like herm, a type of stout animal raised for food back home. She preferred to not eat meat, because she spoke with animals. Eating what one considered to be a friend wasn't the most appetizing. But here she'd eat what was provided and be grateful.

They chewed in silence for a minute or two, until Alex began to drum his fingers on the table. "Theda, have you thought about what I asked last night? About where you came from? I know it's not a comfortable subject, but I want to help. It would be easier if I knew more about your past. Or pretty much anything about you. Are you in danger? Should we reach out to the police?"

"The authorities? Please do not." She kept her tone even, but inside her heart raced. The human authorities were the first place her father would send men. Most Fae in the Earth realm lived on the Dawson University campus secretly owned by her kind, but there were others spread throughout the human realm, and many were connected to the authorities and other high-ranking positions.

"You said when I found you that you weren't in trouble with the police..."

"I am not, but they also cannot help me."

He scratched his head, looking perplexed. "So there's no family or friends you can go to, and the police can't help... Did you have a job?"

A knock sounded at the front door and Theda looked over, thankful for the interruption, but also wary. It could be anyone—including a palace guard in search of her.

A pretty, dark-haired woman with a baby in her arms waved in the window, a bright smile on her face.

Theda's shoulders loosened. This woman was no Fae, though she seemed to take in every detail of Theda and Alex at the table.

Alex groaned and set down his toast. "I spared you from my family as long as possible, but they've arrived. I've got to let my sister-in-law in. I'd like to continue our conversation later, if that's okay?"

Theda didn't answer, because she couldn't lie and she couldn't tell him the truth. Anything she shared about her past put her or Alex in danger.

5

Theda stood as Alex opened the door. The woman who'd peeked in the window stepped inside still holding the baby in her arms and with a small puppy at her feet.

"Alex," she said in a tone that was more of a scold than a greeting. She peered over at Theda. "Hi, I'm Leti."

Alex leaned down and kissed the top of the baby's head. "Theda, this is Leti and my nephew Mateo."

Theda blinked. She'd never seen a man show this kind of affection for a child. Plenty of Fae spent time with their children, and the young ones were very well cared for, but open displays of affection weren't common. She liked Alex's warm nature.

Yet another characteristic to admire about him.

"Nice to meet you," Leti said with a genuine smile.

"Sis, Theda is staying here while she figures some things out. I've gotta go to work. Do you mind helping her with…" Alex glanced over. "Is there anything you need, Theda?"

"I could use different clothes," Theda suggested. Her court clothes would have stood out dramatically on Earth, but her commoner clothes did not blend in either. Both Alex and Leti wore the same type of dark blue pants in a thick fabric, along with casual tops. Theda wanted to look human.

"Of course," Leti said, scanning Theda. Her brows pinched together, and Theda felt every inch of how much her clothes stood out. The other woman plastered on a soft smile and darted a look at Alex, which Alex appeared to ignore.

He grabbed his beige jacket and tied on his boots. "Okay, then, I'm off. You'll be all right?" he asked Theda. "Remember what I said about staying here?"

He'd said he didn't think it was a good idea for her to wander far, and she was in full agreement. She had no desire to draw more attention. "Yes, I'll be fine. Thank you for the breakfast."

"You're welcome." He smiled, and Theda's heart skipped a beat. He stepped out the door.

Alex was an exceedingly attractive human…and that could not be good if she was to live in his house for a few days.

"So you're Alex's…?" Leti entered the room, allowing her question to dangle.

How would Alex wish her to answer? "Friend," Theda finally said.

The puppy that had entered along with Leti sniffed at Theda's feet. He stared up at her and sat on her foot. He wanted her to pet him, so she sank to her knees and petted his back as he leaned up against her. He was a small puppy, his tiny frame only taking up the length of her fitted boot.

"Lucho, leave Theda alone," Leti said, and shifted the baby in her arms.

"It's okay." Theda rubbed behind the puppy's ears. "I love animals."

"Tony gave him to me after I had the baby. Like I need a puppy to take care of along with a newborn." Leti smiled and shook her head. "My husband is all heart, but he doesn't think things through sometimes. Alex is the total opposite." She peered at

Theda as though waiting for her to agree or disagree, but Theda hardly knew Alex.

When she didn't say anything, Leti glanced down at the dog with a frown. "Lucho is a sweet beagle when he's not chewing apart my shoes."

Theda lifted the puppy's chin. "Lucho, why are you chewing Leti's shoes?" The dog whimpered and dug his muzzle into her lap. "No more shoe chewing." She paused a moment, listening to the puppy—more in images than words, but she understood. "Just because Leti leaves at times, it doesn't mean you can destroy her things. People need shoes to protect their feet." The puppy huffed out a sigh.

"If only dogs could understand us, right?" Leti said with a shaky smile.

"Yes, if only." But Lucho understood. He would not chew any more shoes.

The baby started bobbing in Leti's arms and making *da da* sounds. "Well, look," Leti said. "I don't know what you're doing right now, but you could come over to my place and see what I have in my closet. It's full of clothes I can't wear." Her mouth twisted. "Still haven't lost those last few pounds of baby weight. You're welcome to borrow anything you like, and we can go shopping later." She bit the side of her lip. "I'm a lot shorter than you... but you're really thin." She nodded. "My jeans might work as capris. What do you think?"

"I would appreciate that."

Theda stood and looked at the table of dirty dishes and remembered how Alex had cleaned and put them away last night. Their breakfast had been interrupted, and then he'd left for work. She'd never cleaned dishes before...but Alex didn't have a maid. He'd have to do them when he came home, and it felt wrong to leave them when she was capable of doing it. "Do you mind if I wash the dishes first?"

Leti shook her head. "Not at all. I'll help." She set the baby on the floor, and he promptly crawled to the dog and started petting his head and patting his back a little too roughly.

Lucho took it good-naturedly. He licked the baby's face and the baby squealed in a high pitch, rocking back and forth on his round little bottom.

Theda carried the dishes to the sink and turned on the water, searching for the bottle she'd seen Alex pour soap from last night.

"I've got it," Leti said, and inserted a rubber stopper. She grabbed a dark green bottle from a cabinet beneath the sink and poured soap over the dishes. "I'll wash, you dry, and we'll be done in no time."

With Leti's help, washing the dishes and showing Theda where they went, cleaning up the kitchen went quickly.

They made their way toward Leti's house—mother, baby, puppy, and Fae—and Theda tilted her face toward the sun. With a roof over her head and kind humans helping her, she breathed in the crisp scent of freedom for the first time in her life.

6

After leaving Theda with his sister-in-law, Alex stepped out onto the porch—and ran into Old Bob, whose neck was craned as he peered in through the front window just as Leti had moments before.

"Who ya got in there? She's not living with you, is she?" Alex hesitated a second too long. Old Bob frowned. "Can't let someone move in just because she has the looks of an angel. She needs a rental application. I need to see her credit report. Could be a devil of a girl hiding beneath all them blonde, pretty looks."

Alex mentally rolled his eyes. This was the reason he and his father had taken over running the estate these last ten years. As he'd aged, Old Bob lost some of his sanity and had grown too paranoid. Over everything. But the man meant well and had been extremely good to Alex.

How was he supposed to explain Theda to him? She wasn't his girlfriend or his wife...

But she could be. For simplicity's sake. "She's—my girlfriend. I'm paying the rent, but Theda's living with me."

Alex had never lived with a woman, and it had been a while since he'd had a girlfriend, but he couldn't kick Theda out. This seemed like the best solution. She didn't want people to know where she came from, and Old Bob wouldn't understand someone living with Alex who wasn't one of three things: a roommate, a girlfriend, or a wife. If Alex said she was a roommate, Old Bob would insist on a background check. He couldn't say she was his wife, because of the whole life commitment issue, so that left him one option. Of course, he needed to convince Theda that pretending to be his girlfriend was a good idea.

How had one innocent trip to his tool shed resulted in this?

His family depended on him, and he had a plan: take over his father's responsibilities on the farm and become Old Bob's right-hand man, securing his family's lodging and a place for his father to retire. He would also be able to make sure his brother had steady income, since Tony was a bit of a wild card, and their father would be secure with the small pension Old Bob promised to provide.

"Your girlfriend?" Old Bob said disbelievingly. "Since when do you have a girlfriend?"

Alex frowned. It had been two years since his last girlfriend, but he'd been busy holding down the farm. "Point is, I've got one now. A shipment came in and I need to meet up with one of the foremen. Are we good here, or do you want to meet Theda?" *Please say no, please say no...*

Old Bob kicked the porch railing with the heel of his boot, as though testing its strength. "Maybe some other time. I gotta get going too. Just came by to tell you that I spoke to your father. This summer would be a good time to transfer over his last responsibilities to you." Old Bob's gaze grew wary as he peered once more into the living room. "You think you're up to it? Don't have anything burdening you that would prevent you from running the farm?"

"No, sir. I'm ready to take over. Thank you."

"Good, well"—he held out his hand—"congratulations. Just make sure to stay on the straight and narrow. I don't mind your brother working for me, but I don't trust him to run the place. Wouldn't want to see you doing some of the stupid stuff that kid has done over the years."

Unfortunately, Tony's reputation preceded him. "Tony has changed since he married Leti and had a son. He's a responsible family man now." *When he isn't dragging me to bars.*

Old Bob frowned with the side of his mouth. "Right, well, I better be off." He turned and hobbled down the steps, taking them slow with his bowed legs. Though once he hit the dirt drive, he kicked it up a notch, his pace faster than you'd think for a man of his age.

Everything would be fine. Theda could pretend to be his girlfriend until she got back on her feet.

How much trouble could one woman be?

ALEX RETURNED HOME EXHAUSTED from working a ten-hour day, but anxious to see how Theda was doing. He found her sitting quietly on the couch and looking oddly right in his home. He toed off his work boots. "How was your day?"

She stood and glanced down. Her hands twisted together, though her chin remained tilted up. "Leti gave me clothes."

He took in what she was wearing for the first time. She had on slim jeans that narrowed to the middle of her calves and a simple navy T-shirt that highlighted the paleness of her hair, pulled from its braid and spilling over her shoulder.

He swallowed. Theda was beautiful in regular jeans and a t-shirt that hugged her slim curves. Lord help him if she ever dressed to impress.

Maybe it wasn't such a good idea to call her his girlfriend.

They would need to look like a couple to everyone on the outside. Which meant spending time together. Touching. "You look great," he said, his voice deep and scratchy from his throat having gone dry.

Her cheeks pinkened and she glanced toward the kitchen. "Leti also showed me where to put the dishes."

Alex had been in such a rush to get away from Leti and her questions this morning that he'd left breakfast on the table. "Thanks. I'll make us something for dinner. Pizza okay?"

She blinked, her face blank.

For a moment, he got the feeling she didn't know what pizza was, but that was crazy. "Feel free to turn on the TV while I get it ready."

He moved into the kitchen and grabbed a frozen cheese pizza from the freezer. He added extra cheese, sausage, and bell peppers while the oven heated. After a minute, he glanced up and saw Theda staring at the dark TV, biting her lip.

"Let me get that for you. There are a couple of different remotes. I should have shown you how to use them."

Alex walked over and grabbed the two remote controls. He turned on the television and flipped through channels. What would a girl like Theda watch? Not that he knew what kind of person she was, since she wouldn't share anything about herself. He sighed. Sports weren't typically high on most women's lists, which was what he'd normally select. Instead, he chose a popular reality dating show. Not something he'd normally watch, but the women on the farm were always talking about the latest episode.

He handed the controls to Theda and went to check on the pizza. When he turned around, she had taken a seat on the couch. Alex joined her and sat beside her—but not too close. No need to act like a couple when no one was around.

She stared at the screen. "What are those men doing with that woman?"

"Dating her? This is that show where a bunch of guys vie for the attention of one girl. She picks the men she likes, and gets rid of the rest."

"She is with...*all* of them?"

He chuckled. Theda really hadn't seen this show? She must have been living under a rock. "Not all of them. Well, maybe for a while. She dates several of them, letting one or more go home at the end of each episode, until only one man is left. Then they decide if they want to get married."

Theda held up her hand. "The woman decides whom she marries?"

Alex stared at the side of her face. The look she held was one of astonishment. "That's usually how it's done, reality show or not." He was beginning to truly worry about where she came from and how they'd treated her.

She glanced down and fidgeted with her new top. "Oh yes. Of course. I've just never watched this one before."

Of course. But Alex didn't believe it.

The buzzer for the pizza went off, preventing him from asking the probing questions he wanted to address. He pulled the pan from the oven with a towel and cut the pizza into slices, still thinking about Theda and what she might have been through. Of what could have forced a young woman to leave her home and sleep in a shed.

He loaded two plates with pizza and grabbed a couple of beers, then set the food and drinks on the coffee table.

She smiled. "Thank you."

They watched the dating show and drank their beers in relative silence, Alex only moving to grab another beer.

"Why would the woman choose that man?" she said indignantly.

He shook his head and chuckled. The guy the girl had chosen was a douche. "Who knows? His sculpted pecs?" he said. Theda's eyes dropped to Alex's chest and his smile died.

Her cheeks went rosy as her gaze moved from his chest to his shoulders and arms.

He took a deep swig of his beer. Theda shouldn't look at him

40

like that. She *really*, really shouldn't. What was she trying to do? Get him to kiss her? Because it was working. He wanted to kiss her. And she appeared completely unaware of the response her heated looks had on him.

He stood and grabbed their plates, finishing off his beer at the sink while he attempted to get his body to cool down. He wasn't the aggressive caveman type. But right now, he felt like one... "Theda, it's getting late. I don't mean to make you move, but you're sort of sitting on my bed."

"Oh." She stood quickly. "I'm sorry. I'll return to the bedroom. Thank you for the pizza and the dating show."

And now he felt like an ass. She was sweet. He needed to stop thinking about kissing her. It was that damn conversation with Old Bob this morning about how long it had been since he'd dated anyone. Which reminded him...

"One more thing before you head back. I—uh—sort of told my landlord that you're my girlfriend. He wouldn't understand why someone was living with me unless I came up with a good reason. He started asking questions about where you came from, and I know you're not comfortable talking about that right now. I hope that was okay?"

"Yes, but what is—that is to say—what do you mean, your girlfriend?"

He held up his hands. "Oh, it's not what you're thinking. We'll just pretend we're like those people on the dating show. We might need to go on dates, or hold hands sometimes when people are around. That sort of thing."

Her brow furrowed.

Shit. He felt as sleazy as the douche on the show. "I'm sorry. It's the only way, unless you want to have my landlord run a background check on where you came from—"

She quickly shook her head before he could finish. "I am a girl who holds your hand from time-to-time," she said slowly. "Yes, that will be fine."

"Also, we might want to tell my family that you're my girl-friend too. Could be the safest explanation all around. After we found you in the shed, Tony was halfway to believing you are anyway. My brother has a big mouth. I wouldn't put it past him to let the truth slip." Alex had dodged his brother all day to avoid talking about Theda, and it hadn't been easy.

"I understand."

He meant to turn away, but his gaze landed on her mouth instead. Even if it was just handholding, the thought of touching Theda had his mind going in the wrong direction.

"Good night," she said.

"Good night," he answered after the door had already closed.

This was a bad idea. But he'd committed to helping her, and he'd keep his word.

7

The girlfriend ruse Alex had made up sounded like a precursor to the kind of union from which Theda had escaped. Regardless, she had no reputation to uphold in this land. And literally speaking, she was a girl who was a friend—albeit a new friend—so it wasn't a lie.

Unlike in Tirnan, Theda could date as many men as she chose, just as the woman did on the show she and Alex had watched hours ago. But Theda didn't think she'd enjoy kissing multiple men. Only one man piqued her interest, and she was already his unofficial girlfriend.

Did she truly find herself attracted to a human? She imagined Alex's lips and what it would be like to kiss him and her face grew warm, her belly tightening.

It seemed she did.

There was no one here to stop her from enjoying intimacies with a man. She was her own woman in the Earth realm, and she could kiss whom she pleased. Even the handsome human she was living with.

What harm could it do? If anything, it would give her perspective after the water-serpent kisses Adelmar had subjected her to.

Theda rose from the bed with the moon still up, unable to relax. It had been hours since she returned to the bedroom. Alex was surely asleep. There was no need to worry he'd see her in only the white shirt he'd lent her if she snuck out to use the bathroom.

She opened the door quietly, careful not to wake him.

No sound or movement came from the direction of the living room. Confident Alex was asleep, she quickly stepped across the hall and leaned her hip into the bathroom door that seemed to be stuck closed. Until the door swung open.

Theda stumbled forward—and crashed into Alex.

Her hands gripped the thick muscles of his bared arms as she tried to regain her balance. And then she froze.

Alex wore nothing over his chest. He was all smooth skin, and the scent of soap and clean man hit her. She stared at the muscles that rippled down his chest, creating defined ridges and valleys. Her stomach hitched in the odd way it had earlier when she'd thought of kissing him, and her breaths came out short and gasping.

There was a time she'd glimpsed a Fae soldier bared to his waist. A portal had been breached, and the man had been wounded in the abdomen. Alex's chest and arms were more defined than those of the soldier whose job it had been to fight and protect her.

How did a human man grow so muscular?

She forced her eyes up. "I was going to get water."

Alex's eyes lingered on her lips, his hand still supporting her lower back, where it had landed when she'd fallen into him. He seemed to shake his head lightly. "Of course."

He lowered his hand and stepped aside—wider than he needed to—as though he was afraid to touch her again. He stared at her in a strange way.

Did she look that terrible in the middle of the night? Was her hair a fright?

Probably.

She walked into the bathroom and closed the door, sinking her back against it. She'd wanted to lean forward and press her lips to his bare chest. What was wrong with her? She'd made a fool of herself, leaving her room without wearing her day clothes.

Grabbing one of the small paper cups stacked neatly on the sink, she quickly filled it with water and stared at her reflection in the mirror.

Her hair was definitely a fright.

She tried to smooth down the strands, but it looked like she'd been in a windstorm. No use attempting to compose herself when she was only going back to bed.

Theda exited the bathroom and glanced toward the living room. Alex's bare foot hung over the edge of the couch. *That couldn't be comfortable.*

He'd given up so much in order to help her. At some point, he'd insist on knowing more than she was willing to tell him, and she didn't know what she would do.

She scrambled into the bedroom and attempted to sleep, though all she could think about was the man in the other room.

STILL SHAKEN the next morning after running into Theda in the middle of the night wearing nothing but his T-shirt, Alex poured himself an extra-strong cup of coffee. It had taken hours before he'd fallen asleep after that unexpected encounter. With her beautiful hair tousled and her face flushed, it had required all of his self-control to walk away.

His primary focus these last two years had been work, but he remembered a thing or two about what to do when a gorgeous woman crossed his path. He'd had to reel in every instinct so he didn't pull her into his arms. He couldn't take advantage of the beautiful woman he was supposed to protect.

Which was why he'd risen early, set out cereal for her, and done what any sane man would—raced out the door before she woke.

Now he was back home and showering, and realizing his plan to pretend Theda was his girlfriend in order to get his landlord-boss off his back might not be so brilliant. Not only was he thinking about her in a romantic way—which, if he was honest, had crossed his mind a time or two before then—but he'd lied to Leti and Tony too. He'd stopped off at Tony's to ask Leti to swing by and check on Theda later, and they'd asked if she was his girl-friend. He'd simply nodded and turned toward his Jeep before they could pester him for more details. But not before Tony had shouted, "Double date at your place tonight. We'll bring the Chinese food."

Alex had groaned, but he'd walked on and raised his hand in silent agreement. What else could he do? He wanted to protect Theda, and the best way to do that was for her to have a legitimate reason to live with him.

But all day Alex had fought off thoughts of her gorgeous eyes and the mile of smooth, pale skin he'd glimpsed below her nightshirt last night. It was a good thing he was a decent multi-tasker, or he could have lopped off an arm while showing one of the new employees how to properly operate the farm equipment.

So he'd run from her this morning and spared himself an awkward confrontation. He couldn't run every time he found himself attracted to her—which seemed to be constantly.

Theda wasn't trying to seduce him. She appeared innocent, actually, based on their conversation last night about the woman dating more than one guy.

All the better. He didn't want to envision her with other men.

He liked her loyalty. But it also impressed on him the need to keep his distance. Too close and he might do something they'd both regret. He never wanted Theda to feel uncomfortable around him. And using their proximity to try and kiss her when she needed a safe place to live would be wrong.

He rubbed his damp hair one last time with the towel and pulled on a clean shirt. Theda wasn't home yet from Leti's, so he'd taken the opportunity to get cleaned up. He wore a button-down for his "double date," which was what he would do if it were an actual date. Better for keeping up appearances and all that.

Alex entered the living room and turned on low music before striding into the kitchen to open the bottle of red wine he'd picked up on his way home from work. He preferred beer, but he thought Theda might like wine.

The front door creaked open as he was setting out glasses, and Theda walked in, wearing the outfit she'd borrowed yesterday from Leti. Lucho, Leti's dog, trailed at her feet.

He smiled. "How was your day?"

Her gaze scanned down his chest, setting off sparks and heat. His body jerked. How was he supposed to keep it together when she looked at him like that?

She closed the door behind her, seemingly unaware of what her lingering stare did to him. "My day went very well, thank you. I had a wonderful time with Mateo, Leti, and Lucho, of course." She grinned down at the calm puppy at her side.

Which wasn't like Lucho at all. That dog had no manners, and more energy than ten puppies combined.

Alex nodded at the dog. "Did you sedate him? Why's he so well behaved?"

Theda's faced scrunched. "Lucho is a perfect gentleman. Aren't you, Lucho?"

The puppy looked up at her and *woofed*.

Alex shook his head. "Whatever you say. I think he likes you, though." She tried to hide what looked to be a secret smile. Had he said something funny? "Did Leti tell you about tonight?"

He'd told Theda he might need to hold her hand at times, but he hadn't expected to begin the charade this soon.

She smiled. "Yes, our date. What will we do on this date?"

Alex poured her a glass of wine and handed it to her.

She held up the glass in the light, lifting it near her nose, and then took a sip. Her eyebrows rose. "This is wonderful."

"I wasn't sure if you were a red or white person…" He left the comment dangling, desperate for anything about her, but she didn't take the bait.

She dropped to pet Lucho, avoiding an answer.

"Tonight we'll mostly hang out. Maybe watch a movie after we eat the takeout Chinese food Tony and Leti are bringing over. Does that sound okay?"

"Yes, but…" She glanced at her clothes. "I should change. Come on, Lucho. Let's get dressed." Theda took another sip of the wine as she walked away, smiling shyly when he caught her glancing back at him.

When she closed the door to the bedroom, Alex let out a deep breath. Everything would be fine. His boss believed she was his girlfriend, which left him room to help her. She was okay with the date, and she seemed to be making friends with Leti. Even the damn dog loved her.

A few minutes later, she stepped out, wearing a short green sundress that matched her eyes. Her hair was pulled into a low ponytail and her lips had a sheen to them, as though she'd applied lip gloss.

Theda's eyes twinkled at Alex as he blatantly stared, unable to take his gaze off her, and perfectly aware he might be drooling.

He was in trouble. Big trouble.

8

Once Alex managed to peel his eyes off his beautiful houseguest, the evening ended up being one of the most relaxing and enjoyable nights he'd had in a long time.

He and his brother bantered while Theda and Leti chatted about the baby and Lucho. Everyone wolfed down the Chinese food, including Theda who had even asked for seconds. Tony, of course, stuck his nose into Theda's business and asked her about her family. She dodged going into detail by mentioning her brother and saying he lived far away.

Before Alex knew it, Leti and Tony were bussing their dishes and walking out the door to pick up Mateo from Alex and Tony's dad, who could win a grandfather of the year award with his baby-whisper techniques for putting Mateo to sleep.

Alex shut the door behind them, not wanting the night to end, but also knowing he was walking a fine line where is attraction to Theda was concerned. "Would you like to watch a movie?"

She looked over her shoulder and smiled as she rinsed out her wineglass. "I would love to."

He loved how natural she looked in his kitchen. Which was a

first. In the past, it made him cringe if a woman looked too comfortable in his place. But not with Theda.

Alex turned on the television, flipped through channels, and hit the premium stations he subscribed to for movies. "What are you in the mood for? Action/adventure?" *Please say yes.* "Horror?" He'd settle for that too. "Or romantic comedy?" *Say no. No would be the safest.*

Theda's eyebrows pinched in concentration. "I think I would enjoy the romantic movie."

Shit. Shouldn't have offered it. "Sure, let me find the newest release."

They settled on the couch as the movie cued up, and Alex made sure to keep his distance from her.

Unfortunately, his attraction to her spanned the large gap between them. He stretched out his legs and let out a slow breath.

Somehow, after hours of strained movie-watching on Alex's part, he survived through to the end.

How had he managed to go two years without a steady girl-friend? All of a sudden he felt like a powder keg about to explode.

It was Theda. She was different.

He turned off the television and stretched his arms above his head. "I should probably go to bed."

She looked over with a smile that wasn't at all sweet. It was a bit heated and a lot naughty. Alex froze.

She was seriously testing his willpower, and he didn't think she even realized it.

"Come on." He grabbed her hand and nearly hoisted her from the couch in his urgency to get them into separate rooms. "Do you need anything?" Even as he hurried her to the bedroom, he couldn't seem to let go of her hand. "More water? A new nightshirt?"

The nightshirt. Images of Theda in his white T-shirt filled his head. She was his height, and though the T-shirt was baggy on her, it had barely reached her thighs. *Shapely thighs...*

He blinked away the images. They were slowly breaking him.

At the bedroom door, Theda stopped and stared into his eyes. Her gaze dropped to his mouth, and alarms went off in his head. As though he were watching a movie in slow motion, she leaned forward and pressed her lips to his.

He was a statue. Couldn't move, even if he wanted to. She was kissing him, and there was no way he could put a stop to it. His body—and maybe even a piece of his heart—wanted it too badly.

The kiss was innocent and over as soon as it started.

"You shouldn't do that." Was that his gruff voice?

She glanced away, her face turning red. "I'm sorry. I won't do it again."

He thrust his fingers through his hair. "No, it's not that. It's just, we're living together, and you're a beautiful woman. I'd feel like I was taking advantage of you."

"But *I* kissed *you*. That makes it different, does it not?"

He shook his head. He'd lost his damned mind. Because this was beginning to sound like a good idea.

She wet her lips in a nervous gesture, which dragged his gaze down to her full, ripe mouth. "You are kind, hardworking, and... physically appealing."

"You like the way I look?" The words came out before he could stop them. To the memories of women from his past who'd only wanted him for the way he looked or for what he could provide.

She hesitated, seemingly unaware of the turmoil going on inside his head. "It's more than that. I do like the way you look, but where I'm from most people are beautiful. You are appealing in a different way."

And just like that, the bad memories faded and reality set in. Theda was stunning and poised. And she'd never clung to him or acted as though she were using him. It was why he'd felt comfortable offering her his home, and why he liked having her here.

Her gaze flickered briefly away. "And you smell nice," she said. "Like fresh air from the forests I hail from. I like the way your eyes shine when you look at me, and the way your mouth turns up more on one side than the other when you see something you like." Her gaze landed on his lips. "I wish to…"

"Yes?" He waited with bated breath. He'd become one of those tools from the dating show. But who cared. Whatever she wanted —whatever she asked for—he'd give it.

Theda would never use him. There wasn't an ounce of insincerity about her. He didn't know why he'd doubted how right this was. He'd wanted to protect her, but if she wanted more…

She leaned over and pressed her lips to his neck, and he lost all resistance.

Alex wrapped his arms around her back and kissed her cheek, his lips sliding to her mouth where he covered it, showing her how much he'd been dying to kiss her.

A tiny sound erupted from the back of her throat when he gently sucked her bottom lip. She sighed and moved closer, melting into him. He grabbed her hips, pressing them flush with his body, and she moaned.

That was all the encouragement he needed.

He swept her up and into his arms. She was nearly as tall as he was, but incredibly light and delicate.

He carried her to the bed blindly, kissing her neck and the top of her chest exposed by the sundress she wore. The gold necklace she never seemed to remove draped into her cleavage, forever hidden from his eyes. She smelled like wildflowers and spring, and he thought he'd drown in her scent.

He gently laid her across the bed and climbed up beside her where he could touch the curve of her hip. "Do you want to stop?" he whispered hoarsely.

"No," she said, and slipped her hand beneath his shirt, touching his chest and sliding her soft, curious fingers down his stomach.

When she reached his waistband, he lightly grabbed her wrist. "Theda, is this really what you want?"

"Yes. I've never wanted a man, but I want you."

He leaned back, some of the sense her kisses had knocked from his head returning. "What do you mean, you've never wanted a man? Have men forced themselves on you?"

Even the thought caused anger to rise inside his chest.

"No, of course not. I simply meant I've never wanted"—her gaze ran down the length of him—"to see a man's body. To feel him above me. To touch him and have him touch me—"

He closed his eyes. "I think I've got it," he said in a strained voice. He looked down at her. "Have you...have you ever been with a man?"

She shook her head.

Alex clenched his hand at his side. "We can't do this. You're here because you're running from something that terrified you. I want you, Theda, never doubt it. But I don't want to rush this."

9

Theda had been taught by Fae elders and her family that nothing good came from intimacy with a human... But she was beginning to understand the temptation.

Alex left her room, but not before he'd driven her mad with his touches and kisses. She'd never experienced the storm of sensation that was attraction. She wanted it to last, but Alex had pulled away.

Her pulse still pounded and her body ached for his touch, but slowly she was able to think more rationally.

He had used more restraint than she. Never would a man in her realm have refused her; she was a princess. She would have given Alex her virtue, yet he had held back for fear they were going too fast. Perhaps they were, but with every fiber of her being it felt right to be with him.

Theda hadn't seen a single one of her kind since she'd arrived in the Earth realm, but there was no guarantee the reprieve would last. And she didn't want to miss a moment with Alex.

Her thoughts left her restless and unable to sleep for at least an hour after he'd left, when she heard the sound of talking coming from the living room.

At first, she ignored it, figuring it was simply Leti or Tony stopping by for something. Until she sensed the alarm in Alex's voice.

She quickly got up and dressed, and walked out into the living room. Alex stood there looking out the darkened window, talking on a black device he held to his mouth.

He cursed in a form of Latin Theda didn't understand, except for the part about a mother. "The sheep are where?"

"The highway," Theda murmured. Right as the sound of Tony's voice came through the black box and said, "They're walking on the damned freeway."

Alex glanced back at her, his eyebrows pinched together. He pressed a button on the communicator. "How the hell did they get out?" Then he said, "Never mind. Just grab as many workers out of bed as you can. We'll help Jim gather up his flock. He's been a good neighbor to Old Bob and would do the same for us."

Theda walked out the front door onto the porch, listening to the sounds outside. She heard the sheep. They wanted to wander. And they were following one another, ambling. Many were in the range of the highway Theda had crossed when she'd first arrived.

Without a second thought, she pulled out her sack of allon powder she kept stashed on her at all times, even beneath the nightshirt she wore. She grabbed a pinch and set it in the center of her palm. With firm instructions to the sheep, she blew the powder into the air—along with her words.

Scratching noises, like those from the black communicator, came from behind. And Theda realized Alex had followed her out. She turned around suddenly.

He was staring at her.

What had she done? How would she explain her actions?

"Alex, you there?" Tony's voice rang clearly through the speaker. "You're never gonna believe this, but the dumb things turned around. They're headed back in the direction of Jim's property. I've got a couple of guys out here with me. We'll keep an eye on them and make sure they make it back, but I don't think we need to call in all hands. This one seems to have fixed itself."

Alex took a step down from the porch and sat heavily on one of the steps. He set the device next to him and stared at his hands, his expression controlled.

Theda quickly put away the powder. She couldn't lie. She could avoid, but Alex was intelligent; she wouldn't be able to hide what he'd witnessed. She walked over and sat beside him.

Without looking at her, he asked, "Did you do something to make them come back?"

"Yes."

"Will you explain it to me?"

She swallowed and stared off. "No."

She couldn't explain Fae magic. It was complicated even for her kind. Some possessed elemental abilities—power over nature's elements—and others were able to manipulate the mind. But Theda didn't want to tell Alex any of this. The more he knew, the more danger she put him in. He shouldn't know anything about her kind. And if Fae nearby noticed the slight burst of power she'd released to help the herd... She couldn't think of it, it would only increase her worries.

Alex didn't press her further, but she could tell it bothered him as he quietly stood and walked back inside the house, murmuring something about getting sleep.

What she'd done, no human should be able to do. She was different. So far, he hadn't demanded answers, but how long would that last?

When Theda finally fell asleep that evening, she dreamt of her family—and of a guard tracking her relentlessly in the Earth realm.

WHEN ALEX GOT HOME from work the next day, it was to find Theda sitting at the kitchen table chatting with his father.

His dad rose. "That's my cue to leave." He gave Alex a thumbs-up as he passed and walked to the door.

Alex stared at his father's back, waiting for him to close the door before turning to Theda. "Why was he here?"

"Your father came over and introduced himself."

Right. Alex should have done that. He wasn't playing his boyfriend role very well. Though he'd made a damn good show of it last night with the good-night kiss.

"Your father is very proud of you. We talked about you and the farm." She glanced down. "Farming is a common occupation where I come from."

He removed his jacket, setting it on the hook near the door. He didn't speak for fear she'd stop talking. He wanted to know everything about her. Especially after what he'd witnessed last night. He didn't know how she'd done it, but she'd somehow made those animals turn around and return home.

There was no way he and Tony and a handful of workers would have been able to capture the entire flock wandering the freeway before one of the animals got hurt or killed, but Theda had saved them in seconds. It was incredible and terrifying at the same time. Because he'd fallen for her a little bit more last night, and he had no idea who she was.

She was different. He'd always known it. Different because of the way he'd felt about her from the start, and how quickly those feelings had grown. But also different for other reasons she wouldn't explain. She was from some place he never could quite picture in his mind, and now he suspected something really out there. A different planet?

Shit, what the hell was he thinking? He didn't know, but she wasn't like him or anyone else. And he didn't want to see her hurt because of the place she'd run from, or the things she could do.

Theda was working her way into his life, whether he wanted it or not, and he knew nothing about her. How would he find her if she up and left?

When she didn't offer more about her people, he asked, "Can you talk about where you came from now?"

She glanced away. "No."

He rubbed a hand down his face. "Don't keep your past bottled up. If you aren't comfortable talking to me, at least talk to Leti."

She looked up pleadingly. "I cannot talk to *anyone*. I'm sorry, Alex."

"Why? How bad can it be?"

Her face hardened and her chin rose. "You have no idea what you speak of."

He threw up his hands in exasperation and a little anger. "Exactly, I don't. And I want to. I want to understand how you talked to those sheep last night. Because you did talk to them, didn't you?"

Instead of answering, Theda stormed to the bedroom.

Alex considered walking after her, then thought better of it.

He turned and left the house without bothering to grab his jacket. He climbed into his Jeep. He didn't know where he was going, just out. Away. Because the more time he spent with Theda, the more he fell for her, and he couldn't fall for her if he didn't know who—or *what*—she was.

10

Two weeks went by, with Alex and Theda getting into a rhythm that involved a lot of avoidance. She'd asked Leti to teach her how to cook, and when Alex was at work, Theda spent her days helping Leti with the baby and learning the basics of preparing food. It seemed boiling water and toasting bread were two more things the place she'd come from either didn't have, or simply hadn't taught her.

If Alex had to guess, he'd swear she'd been trapped in an underground bunker her entire life. But that didn't seem right. And now he suspected things he couldn't voice. Aliens? Some sort of magic? All he knew was that he cared about Theda. Really cared, which was why he couldn't push her. She didn't want to tell him, and he had to respect her wishes.

As far as Alex knew, Theda hadn't spoken to any more animals, though he was suspicious of her relationship with Lucho. That dog was far too well behaved around her.

Alex couldn't believe he was even thinking about his beautiful houseguest talking to animals, but he knew what he saw. And none of it mattered because it didn't change the way he felt about her.

They'd stopped spending time together when they didn't have to, which made Alex realize how much he'd enjoyed her presence before their fight. It had been damned awkward the one night Tony had stopped by and Alex put his arm around Theda's shoulders. For appearances only, of course, but it had felt like electricity shot down his body where they touched.

Work had been a long one. He walked in the front door expecting to hear female chatter, but the house was silent. "Theda?"

No answer. She must be with Leti.

Instead of taking off his jacket, Alex grabbed a beer, went out onto the porch, and leaned his shoulder against a post. He popped the cap off his bottle. What was he going to do? Theda had him twisted up inside. He wanted so badly to help her, and she wouldn't let him in.

He swallowed a large, cool gulp of beer. This was his favorite time of the day, twilight turning into evening with the sky a purplish blue, the trees shadowed. Only tonight he couldn't relax, and it wasn't simply what he didn't know about Theda. Something felt off.

He pulled out his cell phone to call Leti and Tony and see if Theda was with them—when he heard her.

Or sensed her.

Theda was crying out, but not into the night. Her voice was in his head.

Panic filled his chest, his heart beating a mile a minute. He abandoned the beer and leapt off the porch, racing through the fields. He didn't know how he knew, but Theda was in trouble.

He sprinted for ten minutes straight into the fields, sweat pouring down his temples. He skidded to a stop near a ditch, his head swiveling around, searching, but he didn't know where she was, he only knew she was out here somewhere.

Going on instinct, he raced for the shed where he'd first found her. Why? No good reason. But she had to be there. Every sense he possessed told him she was.

Half a mile later, the sky was even darker, but not dark enough to hide the two figures wrestling in the dirt. The larger one hauled the smaller one up, and that was when Alex realized Theda was being held against her will by one of the biggest men Alex had ever seen.

SHE'D SOUGHT REFUGE. A moment away from the strain that seemed to fill every moment she spent with Alex now, and even the moments in between. Theda wanted so desperately to get closer to him, but after he'd witnessed what she could do with animals, she didn't dare. So she went for a walk, returning to the place where it had all begun.

Theda found the shed where she'd first met Alex a mile or two from his house. It was locked, and she smiled, remembering how surprised he'd been when he first found her there.

Things were so tense between them these days. They couldn't go on ignoring one another. She was learning to cook from Leti and had found ways to help around the house, but that wasn't enough. It wasn't fair to Alex. She needed to find her way in this world without relying on his kindness.

She stared out at the deep blue sky, growing darker as the minutes passed, knowing she must leave and not liking the idea. Not when it meant leaving Alex.

And then she sensed something.

Not something. *Someone.*

She spun around, staring into the fields.

Just beyond the shed, a man stepped out of a copse of trees, and Theda's heart nearly stopped in her chest. Then she was running.

She didn't get far before a large body slammed into her. She fell, her face and arm skidding across the dirt and gravel, his weight cutting off her air supply.

"At last, you are on your own," the Fae said near her ear. "I worried I might need to expose myself to get to you, and then murder your little friends. I wouldn't have minded if it weren't so messy to clean up."

Theda bucked to get him off, but he was twice her weight. And not just any Fae, but a tracker. Her nightmare had come true. "Let me go," she said, gasping.

He flipped her over and pinned her hands above her head, pressing down his larger frame against hers. "Never. Have you any notion how long it took me to find you?" He tore the bracelet her brother had given her off her wrist and tossed it away. "Your little trinket might have hidden you, but once you used your magic, you were mine. It was only a matter of time."

She'd acted impulsively, saving the animals for Alex. But she'd wanted to help, and now this man would return her to Tirnan. She'd worried about staying longer with Alex, being a burden, and now all she could think about was getting back to him.

Theda tried to free one of her hands. She'd brought her knife with her; she always did when she left the house. But it was in her boot and she couldn't reach it.

The tracker's eyes narrowed. He had a deep scar down the side of his pale face. Fae didn't scar unless they'd suffered months of deprivation and were attacked with magic.

He gripped both of her wrists with one hand and patted down her body—touching her in a way that made her stomach lurch. "Much as I'm enjoying this, you could spare me the effort and tell me where you've hidden your weapon."

"What weapon?" She feigned ignorance.

His mouth twisted and he slid his hand down both of her legs until he freed the dagger from her boot. "There she is." He tucked the dagger behind him, presumably in a pocket, and slipped something around her wrists. Shackles made of magic and glowing a vibrant blue.

He hauled her up, but before he could straighten, she swung her locked wrists over his head and kneed him in the face with all her might.

The tracker grunted and Theda ran. Until he tackled her again. But this time, she twisted quickly and slid halfway out from under him. And then she heard it.

Alex, calling to her.

She looked in the direction the tracker did, to see Alex running full tilt toward them.

The tracker moved, and Theda grabbed her knife from where he'd tucked it in his belt. She stabbed him in the side a second before he knocked the blade from her hands and gripped her neck.

And then Alex was there and leaping on top of the tracker. He knocked the Fae to the side and off Theda.

She didn't know what power the tracker possessed, but all Fae had something. And this man was much larger than Alex.

The tracker elbowed Alex in the stomach, forcing him back. Then he cracked his large fist across Alex's jaw, dropping him to his knees.

Theda went to grab the dagger in the dirt several feet away, but the tracker locked his arm around her waist before she could get past him, hauling her into the air. "You'll be coming with me."

"No!" Alex shouted, looking up from where he'd fallen, his dark eyes desperate.

"It's okay," she said. The Fae would kill him; there was no doubt in her mind. She couldn't let that happen. Not to *this* man. "It was inevitable things would end this way."

The tracker waved his hand in front of him in the shape of a square. A second later, the air wavered. He had the power to make portals. Convenient for him, not so much for her.

It was over. She'd be returned to her father. Likely married off to Adelmar after she'd faced whatever punishment her father deemed adequate. But it had been worth it. *Alex* had been worth it.

Instead of stepping through the portal like she expected, though, the tracker suddenly lurched to the side.

She looked up and saw blood dripping from his mouth. Theda slid to the ground as his grip loosened and he fell away from her entirely, blood pouring from his back.

Alex stood behind them, his hand holding the dagger and shaking.

The tracker wasn't moving, and the electric-blue shackles around her wrists sputtered and disappeared. That could mean only one thing.

Alex had killed him.

Few things killed Fae. But beheadings and direct strikes to the heart could.

Theda threw her arms around Alex's neck, holding him tightly. He didn't say anything, simply dropped the knife and held her too, his arms bands of steel keeping her upright.

"Will there be more?" he finally asked.

"I don't know. I—I don't think so. Trackers usually travel alone. It's more efficient." She let him go and grabbed her bracelet from the ground where the tracker had thrown it, putting it back on her wrist. "They're not easy to catch off guard. He underestimated you."

"No," he said. "He underestimated the lengths I'd go to protect you."

He pulled her close and kissed her for the first time in weeks, and she kissed him back as though she were starving. Because she was. Starving for him. She never wanted to leave Alex. She'd work it out—find a way to make herself useful and safe, and stay with him.

Last night, Alex had put his conscience aside and buried the body near the shed. He'd killed a man—or what he thought to be a man. But it was either kill him, or lose Theda to who knew what fate.

He'd slept curled around her on his bed, both of them fully clothed. He'd been too afraid to ask her where the man had come from. Afraid her answer would make what was building between them impossible.

He held her and kissed her forehead before leaving for work. "Will you be okay?"

"I think so. No one else has come, and they would have by now if the tracker were working with others. It's unlikely he told anyone he'd found me. They get paid per job. He wouldn't have wanted to share the spoils."

"Jesus." Alex scrubbed a hand down his face.

"How did you know?" she asked.

"Know what?" His shoulders were tense with worry. Maybe he should stay home. Call in sick.

"That I was in trouble."

Good question. "I heard you."

"Heard me?"

"You were calling me and I heard you."

She shook her head. "I wasn't able to use the powder. I didn't call to you."

He lifted his eyebrow. "Powder?"

"Alex, the things I can do... It's complicated. Will you trust me that it's better if you don't know?"

"I wish you trusted me enough to share it."

She twined her fingers with his. "I trust and admire you more than anyone. I would tell you if I could, but it's safer for both of us if I don't."

He kissed her softly again, this time on the lips. A shot of electricity zoomed down his spine, lighting up his body with want. She swayed into him. "Should I stay home today?" he asked, hoping she'd say yes and give him a reason to skip responsibility and spend the day with her.

"Go to work. I'll visit Leti. Everything will be okay."

Reluctantly, Alex left, but he worried about Theda the entire day. He called Leti to check in, but really, he just wanted to know Theda was safe.

When he got home that evening, Theda was already in the kitchen, and the scent of meat filled the room. Burnt meat.

"Everything okay?" he asked.

She glanced over her shoulder, looking harried. "I—No. I've been cooking, but it seems I've done something wrong. The meal doesn't smell right."

He toed off his boots and moved into the kitchen, opening the oven door. A rush of steam and smoke hit him in the face and he shut the door partway and opened the kitchen window. "I think I see what the problem is." He pointed to the stovetop where the oven knobs were, and switched them off. "You set it to broil, when you should have turned it to bake. What were you trying to make?"

Theda licked her lips nervously. "Leti said you liked steak. She showed me how to bake, and I thought..."

He smiled gently. "Thank you." Theda hadn't said as much, but he got the sense she wasn't a big fan of meat. Yet she'd tried to make him a steak because she knew he loved it.

He pulled out the pan, now that the smoke had wafted away, and set it on the stove, scratching his jaw. "We could still eat—"

"No." Theda shook her head, laughing. "Please. I don't think I could." She scrunched her nose.

He smiled, chuckling, because she had an adorable belly laugh.

After a moment, she looked over and her smile faded. Her eyes dropped to his mouth.

He swallowed and looked away. Didn't matter her past or what she could do; she had an effect on him he couldn't deny. "I'll go out. Get us something to eat."

"May I come with you? I don't want to be alone after last night, if that's okay?"

"Of course. I'd rather you not be by yourself until we're certain no one else will come. That is, if you want to stay here? You're not trapped at my house, or with me, Theda."

A sultry smile spread across her mouth before he could blink —before he even thought she knew what she was doing. "I'm here because I want to be with you."

Alex gripped his neck. "Come on. Let's get some air." *A lot of cold, cold air.* What was he going to do with her?

He didn't recognize himself anymore. The lengths he was willing to go to protect and be with her were extreme.

They drove into town and stopped at the local pizza joint. Theda glanced around nervously, her hand wrapped around the gold bangle she wore on her wrist. Now that Alex thought about it, she never seemed to take it off, along with the necklace she wore. "You okay?" he asked.

She tried to give him a reassuring smile. "Yes. Fine," she said, but he sensed her nervousness. He was nervous too. Would more people like the tracker come looking for her?

They got out of the car and he put his hand on her lower back, guiding her to the restaurant. They put in a to-go order, but it would take thirty minutes to cook. He should have thought about that before they'd left the house. He could have called it in. But at the time, getting out of the confined space, where Theda was looking at him with sultry eyes, seemed more important for his self-control.

He didn't want Theda to leave. That was why he was so adamant about knowing her past. He wanted to know how to protect her. But as long as she was safe, and the man who'd found her last night would never again return, why not forget the past and move forward?

They took a short walk down the block while they waited for their food. An evening farmers' market and small art exhibit were set up in one of the parking lots. They walked through and looked at the displays, and Theda seemed taken by what she saw, a smile on her face.

"What will you do? Will you move on after last night?" He dreaded the answer, but he needed to hear it. To know whether she'd leave him, now that he realized he didn't want her to go.

"I—haven't thought about it. Do you want me to leave?" Her voice was soft, vulnerable.

Alex stopped near a tiered fountain and grabbed both of her hands. "I want you to stay. I thought I needed to know where you came from, but that's bullshit. I don't care about that. I mean, I do, if you want to talk about it or why that man came after you last night. But it's not necessary. I'm here for you. I don't need the past. I just need you."

Theda bit her lip. "I can stay?"

He pulled her to his chest, his hand on the back of her head pressing her near. "Please stay. Be my girlfriend in truth."

"In truth," she repeated. "I've always been yours."

Alex pressed his lips to hers. He could do without just about anything—a home-cooked meal, knowing her past—shoot, he'd even live in that damned shed as long as she was at his side.

He'd never felt this way about a woman.

Somehow they made it home and he even remembered to bring the pizza, but it didn't get eaten. At least, not right away.

Alex was kissing and touching Theda before they made it inside the door. She tugged off their jackets as he tossed the pizza box on the table. His aim must have been off, because he heard it land on the floor.

He didn't care. He wanted her, and this time it wouldn't be him pushing on the brakes.

She was wiggling her way into his heart with her attempts at cooking and the purest, sincerest admission: *I've always been yours.* It was all he'd needed to hear.

If she wanted him to stop, he would, no questions asked. But he was going to show Theda how much he cared, and how she made him feel—the electricity that had sparked from the moment he first saw her.

He cradled her head in both of his hands and leaned back. "You won't leave me, will you?" He felt his brow furrow as he tried to figure out what he was saying. "You fell into my life out of nowhere, and I suddenly have the worst fear of losing you."

She swallowed. "I will never leave you willingly."

That wasn't an answer. It left too many alternatives, but her mouth was back on his, and he forgot what he wanted to say next, because she started unbuttoning her top, revealing pale, silky flesh.

Alex swept his hands over each section of skin Theda exposed, helping her ease her top off, and revealing the large purple gemstone surrounded by diamonds at the end of her necklace. Wherever she came from, she hadn't been poor. Then he took in the rest of her and his mind blanked.

Seeing her in nothing but her jeans and bra—her delicate shoulders, the swell of her breasts—his mouth went dry.

Reaching behind her, he quickly removed the last piece of clothing hiding her from his eyes.

She leaned back a fraction, surprise filling her face. "You did that very quickly."

"Shhh," he said, not wanting to explain how he'd come by that talent. His new motto: Leave the past in the past. "Nimble fingers."

Theda tried to unbutton his jeans, but he undid them for her, and had her jeans halfway down her creamy legs in seconds.

He stood back in his boxer briefs and took in the beautiful woman in front of him in nothing but tiny underwear. "You're stunning." His voice sounded deep and rumbly even to his ears. He wanted Theda. All of her.

She looked away, as though embarrassed, her arms rising to cover herself. "All of us are attractive."

"I don't know what you mean by that, but I think you believe I'm talking about your body." He eased her arms to her sides and touched her collarbone, trailing his hands over her breasts and the slight swell of her lower belly. "Your body is beautiful, but so are you. The way you care about animals, the friendships you've built with Leti and even my dad. They love you, Theda. I'm falling in love with you."

He kissed her with all the pent-up passion that had been gnawing at his insides since she'd stepped into his life. And she seemed to have the same thing in mind, because her mouth was just as determined to prove her affection for him.

He eased her back and her legs hit the mattress. They tumbled down until he was lying over her, bracing his weight on his arms.

"Are you sure you want this?" He couldn't believe he was even thinking about stopping, but this was her first time. He wanted to make sure she was ready.

In answer, Theda reached down his back and slid her hands beneath his boxer briefs, squeezing his ass.

That was a strong sign, but he needed to hear it. "Theda, answer me," he said gruffly, his control slipping.

She reached between them and tentatively touched the length prodding her soft thigh through the thin material he wore. And then she slipped her hand beneath the fabric and ran a finger down him, then two, and then her fist gripped him.

He inhaled sharply and counted to five. She was killing him. In a good way.

"Theda?" His voice came out on a choke.

"Yes, I want this. I want you."

And then her panties flew off. Not really. He tried to act the gentleman, but he was a lot excited and a bit overeager to press her naked body to his.

She pushed his boxers down with her feet—which he found extremely sexy and good improvising for someone who'd never done this before.

His mind paused on that thought. He was going to be her first.

And somehow that was just fine. He would never hurt her. He only wanted to love her.

Their naked bodies finally touched and a gust of breath whooshed from his lungs. He savored the sensation of her skin and soft curves. Nuzzling her neck and running his lips along her hairline, he breathed in her light wildflower scent. And then his mouth was on hers.

Alex wanted to take things slowly, but she was giving him breathy sighs and little moans that had him gripping the blankets beside her head. He didn't want to rush her. He'd touch her all night and be content if that was all she wanted.

But he didn't need to worry, because the second his hand grazed her outer thighs she parted her legs just enough for his hips to slide between those silky, long limbs.

You would think he was the virgin the way his arms quaked. He told himself it was because he'd been holding his weight over her for a good long while, but he was pretty sure it was because he'd never experienced this before. The connection they had was more powerful than love—deeper, stamped in granite, and never to be removed. As though they were always meant to be.

As though he'd simply been waiting for her, biding his time, until his real life could begin.

At this moment, he was damn near ready to propose, but one thing at a time. He didn't want to scare her off.

Theda shifted, and that was all it took for him to penetrate the first inch that had them both moaning. He moved gently with her body, waiting for her to relax and allow him entrance, kissing her and touching her breasts and the sensitive spot at the juncture of her thighs. Her fingers gripped his hair and she shivered. He inched further with each short thrust, until he was fully seated.

"I love you," he whispered.

She rocked her hips, and Alex moved at the feel of her grasping his shoulders and holding him to her, urging him on.

He kissed her neck and squeezed her breast, thumbing her nipple.

Soon, her breath hitched, and her body clamped on his, her back arching as a loud, sexy moan came from her. He held back just long enough until her body stopped quaking before his control slipped and his own orgasm hit him.

He shut his eyes as he caught his breath, because for a second he went blind with the power of his climax. Which was crazy. And wonderful. And all Theda.

He lifted his head and looked at her beautiful face and sated smile.

Kissing her eyelids, her cheeks, he savored the moment. He gave her one last kiss on the lips, assuring himself she was okay, and went to remove the condom. *Shit.* And realized he hadn't put one on.

He'd never forgotten before.

Whatever voodoo that had him racing through the dark last night, hearing Theda's voice from miles away, must have also strung him too far out with lust to think clearly. He'd experienced a moment of complete stupidity.

Alex collapsed beside her and tucked her near. Their relationship was fast, but in the end, it wouldn't matter that he'd forgotten protection. He felt in his heart that Theda was the woman for him.

And what were the chances she would get pregnant the first time anyway?

EPILOGUE

TWENTY-TWO MONTHS LATER...

"She looks like you," Theda said, lying on the floor and smiling at their daughter.

The baby sat on her round bottom and waved a colorful ball with tiny holes for her fingers back and forth. For the moment, Elena was stationary, but the minute her attention wandered she'd be up and walking around like a drunken sailor.

Theda was exhausted from chasing their daughter around all day, but happier than she'd ever been in her life.

Alex quickly toed off his boots and dumped his coat beneath the front door, not even bothering to hang it. He rushed into the kitchen to wash his hands, then plopped down on the floor beside them. "She's way too pretty to look like me. Her hair is darker than yours, but see"—he held up a strand of the baby's hair—"my hair is black and our daughter's is this reddish brown. She gets that from you. And her eyes... She has the most beautiful eyes."

Theda couldn't argue. Elena had inherited both of their traits. She might be biased, but she thought they'd created the most beautiful child inside and out. At one year old tomorrow, Elena was sweet, with such a gentle soul. And with a lot of energy.

When Theda discovered she was pregnant, she was shocked.

How could she conceive so quickly? It was extremely rare among her kind, and she and Alex had only been intimate the one time without precautions to prevent pregnancy. But when Leti had suggested Theda take a pregnancy test, she did as her sister-in-law said. Apparently, Theda's sudden craving for meat in large quantities had tipped off her friend, who was more experienced in these things. Alex and Theda soon discovered the truth.

A daughter. He'd given her a baby girl.

He sniffed. "I think she needs a diaper change."

Theda raised her eyebrow.

"Right." He hid his smile. "My turn."

Whenever Alex came home, he went straight to Theda and their child. He wasn't afraid to change the baby's diapers, and he still cooked for them—mostly because Theda never quite mastered it and burnt more meals than she cared to admit. Fortunately, her daughter mostly ate baby food, and they'd only just started her on regular milk.

Theda leaned over Elena so that the baby could play with her amethyst necklace while Alex made quick work of changing the diaper. As soon as he finished and cleaned up, he grabbed a notepad and leaned against the couch, a lock of black hair falling over his forehead as he studied his daughter with an artist's eye.

He had begun sketching again. She'd noted the sketches in his house when she'd first arrived, but she'd not once seen him create anything. Until she became pregnant with their child. And then her husband sketched nonstop. Landscapes, images of the family —images of Theda, though those had always concerned her.

She'd never stopped worrying that her father would find her, or that another tracker would return. Most of the time, she hid the sketches Alex created of her or destroyed them entirely, though it pained her to do so. She loved everything he created and framed as many of them as she could. But she feared images of her were too dangerous to have around. And whenever a friend or family member wanted to take a picture of her, she always made sure to look down at the baby or turn her head away at the last second.

But the sketches Alex made of Elena—Theda had an entire baby book full of them. One day, she would show them to her daughter.

She shook a plastic rattle Mateo had outgrown above Elena, and the baby climbed to her feet to reach for it.

"Would you like me to make something for dinner?" she asked.

Alex looked up, his eyes telling her everything he was thinking.

She smacked his arm. "Wretched man. I already made something. In the slow cooker. And it's Leti's recipe, so it's safe."

He grinned mischievously. "I don't know. *Slow cookers.* A lot can go wrong when you throw things in a slow cooker."

He was making fun of her. And she loved it. So much so that she tossed his notepad to the side and lunged across his lap, kissing his neck. She'd never tire of her husband's scent—like the outdoors and everything comfortable mixed in one.

Alex chuckled and wrapped his arms around her. "At least our daughter will grow up knowing how much her parents love each other, since you can't keep your hands off me."

She pinched his waist and he laughed some more. "I believe it's the other way around." She gave him a knowing look.

"Last night was definitely all me. It's your fault for wearing that naughty lingerie Leti gave you at the wedding shower."

"It was getting dusty in my dresser drawer. I thought it needed to be aired out."

"Oh, it was aired out, all right—taken off and thrown right into the air the second you slipped it on."

She laughed and kissed his lips. "Everything's set for tomorrow?"

"Pretty sure Old Bob's entire workforce will be there." He kissed her neck and slid his palms up her top. "How will I keep my hands off you until they're gone?"

"By being good, you naughty man."

THE NEXT DAY, the house filled with family and friends to help celebrate Elena's first birthday. Theda never could have imagined such happiness if she hadn't been living it.

"Hand her over, sis. Let me get a snuggle from my little niece." Tony leaned down and cooed in Elena's upturned, smiling face, and Theda handed her daughter to him.

She smiled, watching Elena squeeze Tony's nose. He made a loud honking sound and the baby erupted in giggles.

There was nothing more beautiful than her child's laughter—

A knock sounded at the door.

Theda heard it because of her heightened senses, but it was too loud in the room for anyone else to note. Even Alex, who was gobbling up a slice of cake as he discussed plans for the new irrigation system with his father, hadn't heard the sound.

He looked at her directly, as if he'd sensed her staring, and his mouth broke out into a wide smile. He winked.

Theda's face heated. This man... She'd never known a man could be so kind—and, well, appealing. If they were not playing with their daughter, they were kissing. She wasn't pregnant yet, but at this rate, they'd have another child soon.

Imagine what her father would think if he knew she'd conceived so quickly. If only Fae understood the happiness a union with a human could bring. But Fae believed power and magic were all that mattered.

If her father knew she'd borne a half-human child... A stinging shiver racked her body. He could never know. He'd take Elena and wait to see if she possessed powers. They came from a strong noble line and there was a good chance Elena would grow up to possess a magical ability. And if her daughter did...Theda couldn't think of it. She'd have to prepare Elena once she was older.

Whatever circumstances lay ahead, Theda would protect her daughter at any cost.

The door...

She wiggled past friends and neighbors crowding the small living room, but a sinking feeling settled in her belly. It had been over two years since she'd run from Tirnan, but the fear of being found never quite left her. She'd married, had borne a child, and no one had found her after the tracker. There was no reason to believe someone would today of all days.

She took a deep breath and opened the front door with a smile on her face, expecting another group of friends to have arrived.

But the person at the front door wasn't a friend.

No. NO. Her body turned hot, then ice cold with fear.

Adelmar Lucent stood on the porch in all his arrogant glory. "Hello, Theodora. I've come to take you home."

She'd softened since leaving Tirnan—grown more human, allowing her emotions to show. But she couldn't afford to reveal what she felt right now. "I won't go."

He peered over her head into the room. "You will, or everyone in this dwelling perishes. Is that what you wish?" He snarled down at her. Gone was the handsome courtier who'd at least pretended to admire her once upon a time. "To see your little human friends die in front of you?"

Adelmar could set things on fire—with deadly precision. If he wanted, he could burn each person in the room and not touch a single piece of furniture.

Instinctively, Theda reached for the satchel at her waist, but it wasn't there. Neither was her dagger. She'd stopped wearing them a year ago after the birth of her child. She hadn't wanted the baby to accidentally touch them when she was holding her. "Why?" she asked, unable to stifle the desperation in her voice.

He leaned forward, his long, light brown hair sliding over his handsome forehead. "Because you made me look like a fool," he growled.

"Is that what you want? To marry me? Because—"

"That opportunity has passed," he said sharply. "There will be no marriage for you. Not anytime soon. And not with me. I seek a woman of quality. Not this"—he sniffed, his face twisted in disgust—"disgrace of a female."

"Then why must I return?"

"Because the king, your father, wishes it. Don't make me wait, and don't make me angry, Theda. I just might kill all of these people for the pleasure of it." His pale blue gaze wandered lustfully over the crowd.

Theda swallowed and took a deep breath. She didn't dare look at her husband and child for fear Adelmar would target them. "I will—go with you," she managed to get out. "Will that make you happy?"

He looked down, emotionless. "No. But it will do for now."

"On one condition."

He chuckled darkly. "You truly believe you are in a position to make demands?"

"They"—she turned her head slightly, indicating the crowd behind her—"must not know where I've gone. I don't want them to try to find me."

"Of course not." He huffed. "Humans must never know of our presence. But have you kept it a secret? Are you certain no one knows who you are?"

Theda's mind flashed to her daughter and the potential powers she might possess one day. Even if Theda's ability was considered weak, her daughter's could be powerful. Everyone in the Rainer family line had a powerful ability except for Theda.

Adelmar hadn't mentioned the child. Not once. Which meant he didn't know about her. Or, at least, she prayed he didn't. No one would suspect she'd had a child in such a short amount of time.

"They don't know of Fae," she said, her voice strong and clear.

Her past was the one secret Theda had kept from Alex. And now she must leave him, and he would never understand.

Her throat turned thick with emotion. She had to do this. It was the only way to keep them safe.

"Good." Adelmar tipped his head to the side. "Go to the back bedroom. My men have created a portal on the outside wall. I'll meet you there."

Theda nodded but held the door partway open, blocking the view of her guests. "How did you find me?"

He smirked. "I made friends with an Oldlander in the Earth realm. She was very accommodating. She helped me find all Fae within a five-hundred-mile radius, which was how I learned of the tracker who'd passed through here. We found his body, by the way." He shook his head. "A shallow grave? So disrespectful. It didn't take long to find you after that." He glanced down at her bracelet. "I'm assuming you thought the magical jewelry would keep you safe? Even your muted energy level couldn't hide you once we were close enough."

It had kept her safe—long enough for her to know true happiness.

"We'll find whoever helped you murder the tracker and kill them, you can depend on it."

Her mind raced to Alex. "How could a human kill one of us? I stabbed the tracker."

He scanned her briefly, a glint of admiration in his eyes. "I didn't think you had it in you. If so, his death will be one more item you must atone for. Go back now, and don't hesitate; the portal will not last forever. You know what will happen if you make me angry." He glanced suggestively over her shoulder at her family and friends.

She nodded and closed the door, slowly turning to the crowd. Alex was staring at her, a frown on his face as he made his way over.

He slipped his arms around her waist. "Who was that? You look upset."

It was a testament to how she'd changed since arriving in the Earth realm, and how well Alex knew her, that he could tell her feelings so clearly.

She smiled. "I'm fine." And she would be once she knew her family was safe. "It was only a man wishing to show me his magic tricks."

"Magic tricks? Like a traveling carnie? Here?"

"Something like that. I sent him away."

A sharp pain speared her chest, her stomach roiling. The notion of leaving her husband and daughter was nearly unbearable. But if Adelmar knew of them…he'd have them killed in front of her.

If she could save Alex and Elena, living without them would be worth it.

She leaned up and kissed her husband with all her love, all her passion for him.

His arms tightened on her waist. "After we put the baby to bed —" His brow quirked suggestively.

She smiled in spite of the tears welling behind her eyes. She blinked and shook them off. How could she leave him? "Later," she whispered.

And in her mind, she intended to keep that promise. She would stop at nothing to make sure her family was safe and to return to them.

Theda glanced past Alex. She hadn't much time. "Where's the baby?"

"Charming Tony."

She squeezed Alex's hand and stepped toward their beautiful child, with the dark curls and light eyes that were a mix of her and Alex.

She pulled Elena from the arms of her uncle, who appeared put out that she'd taken the baby while they were having their fun.

They would protect Elena. Alex, yes, but his family too. Even little Mateo cared for the baby and made funny faces to make her laugh. If Theda had to leave, at least she'd be leaving Elena where she was loved. Protected.

To have been given this beautiful family was more than Theda had ever wished for. That she had them for such a short time…

Her hands shook and her body grew even colder. *No,* she'd return. They would be together again—she had to believe that.

Theda nuzzled Elena close, breathing in her baby scent. "I love you," she whispered. "More than you will ever know."

She quickly wiped a tear that had escaped before she handed the baby back to Tony, who had Mateo in one arm and was waiting for Elena to fill the other. Alex had been stopped by Leti, and they were talking animatedly about whether Old Bob would begin paying Alex's father's pension. Legal documents had been drawn up and it sounded like it would happen in the coming year, and then her family's financial future would be safe too.

Theda swallowed and allowed herself one last look at each of them: Tony, Leti, Mateo, and her precious Elena. Her husband she saved for last.

He glanced up, his face still holding signs of concern. But Theda smiled away the worry and walked toward the back bedroom, knowing Alex would soon follow—that he'd seen through her fake smile.

She closed and locked the door behind her.

He couldn't come inside. Not until she'd gone.

She glanced at the exterior wall. A shimmer was present, a sign that the portal had been created—and would not likely last long, since it was only temporary.

Her hands shook, her heart nearly tearing from her chest. She had to do it. *Had to.* She couldn't remain and keep her family safe. But stepping forward drained every ounce of essence she possessed. To leave Alex and Elena might kill her. But this wasn't about her. This was about saving them.

She unclasped her amethyst necklace, the one her mother had given her. The only sentimental piece of her past she'd taken on her way from Tirnan. She set it gently on the nightstand for Elena until she could return. For that was the only thing moving her feet forward—the belief she'd be back.

Grabbing a piece of paper and pencil from the nightstand drawer, she wrote a quick message to her husband.

Alex,

> *They've come for me. Believe me when I say I never could have told you where I come from. It was too dangerous, and now I fear I've brought danger to our home. For the love of our child and what we share, do not try to find me. I will come to you when it is safe. Burn this message and tell no one the little I've shared.*
>
> *I love you with all I have, all I know, and all that I am,*
> *Theda*

She kissed the note, her throat tightening, and set it on Alex's pillow before crossing the room to her sock drawer, where she grabbed her pouch of allon powder. She hadn't dared use it after she'd signaled the tracker last time, but she would use it now.

Taking out a pinch, she whispered a command to Lucho and blew the magical powder into the air. A second later, she heard the dog—so well behaved since she'd arrived—howling in the living room.

A commotion arose outside her bedroom door, and then the telltale sound of the back door closing as Tony or Alex took the dog into the backyard.

"Goodbye, Lucho," she whispered to the sweet dog who'd become her friend, and who'd provided a lifesaving distraction.

Just as the portal began to fade, Theda grabbed one of Alex's sketches of their infant daughter.

The sound of pounding came from the bedroom door, the knob rattling. "Theda!" Alex called.

She squeezed her eyes tight against the urge to go to him, hid the sketch beneath her clothing, and leapt through the portal.

Dear Reader,

I hope you enjoyed *Fates Altered*, the story of how Theda and Alex set a course that would forever change the Fae realm.

Grab the next book in the Halven Rising series, ***Fates Divided***, the full-length story of Elena Rosales, Alex and Theda's daughter.

Elena is the first Halven to become a part of the Fae world, and the transition is deadly.

Grab *Fates Divided* Now!

Cheers,
Jules

FATES DIVIDED PREVIEW

Chapter 1

Elena's hands shook as she burst through the front door and scanned the apartment for her roommate. "Reese!"

No answer.

Reese must still be on campus.

Elena raced into the kitchen and slammed open cupboard doors until she found what she was looking for. She grabbed a metal pot, filled it with water, and placed it on the tile counter across from the fridge—clear away from any potential heat source, like the stove.

It was ridiculous to stare at a pot of water, but to run a true test she needed to repeat what she'd done in class forty-five minutes ago.

A few seconds passed, and then she felt it. The tingling beneath her skin erupted like before, which wasn't reassuring, though she supposed it was good for experimental purposes. She thought about how water molecules reacted when heated, just as she'd thought about the solution's properties in class. By instinct

—the way she'd done with the class chemicals—she ran her hand over the pot.

The water boiled. With nothing to warm it.

Elena flinched as steam billowed up. *Not again. What the hell?* She eased back until she bumped into the fridge, her pulse racing. What was happening?

After a second, she grabbed the handle and tossed the pot into the stainless steel sink before it scorched the tile. Or did something else it wasn't supposed to do.

Leaning forward, she carefully held the back of her hand over the place where the pot had been and sensed the warmth there. She curled her palms around the edge of the counter and gripped hard.

"It's okay." She sucked in a deep breath and let it out slowly. "Everything is going to be *okay.*"

She'd gone straight home to collect her thoughts after her solution had boiled over in class without heat, but she couldn't run an experiment in her kitchen. Something wonky must have gone on with the chemicals in class. Maybe a leftover residue had been stuck to the bottom of the beaker. That didn't explain the water boiling just now, but there *had* to be a logical reason.

Hurrying into her bedroom, Elena grabbed her laptop. She needed to return to ground zero where the liquid anomalies had begun—in a campus lab. There she could access the right equipment for measuring and calculating every step, every nuance, to determine what was making the liquids boil.

Reese stormed into the room, and Elena jumped, startled. Reese plopped onto the bed. "Guess what?"

Elena returned her gaze to the laptop, her shoulders still tense. "Where'd you come from?" She scrolled through the online campus map for an open lab.

But it was no use. All of them were closed, except during class hours. She sank her head onto the desk. How the hell was she going to experiment if she couldn't get inside a lab? Her next class was a week from now, and what if the chemicals did something weird again? She'd managed to hide it from her classmates today. The chances of that a second time were slim.

"I just got home, but listen to this." The bed squeaked as though Reese had shifted closer. "You're going to have to cook me meals for the rest of the school year after what I scored for us."

Reese's words cut through the fog of Elena's distress. She glanced over incredulously. "How is me cooking for you everyday any different from what I do now?"

Reese's expression was pure innocence. "You know I'm not domestic."

"And I am?"

The off-campus dorm they lived in offered meal plans on campus, but that required a two-block trek she and Reese rarely managed without strong motivation.

"At least your aunt taught you how to cook," Reese said. "My mom paid people to do that stuff. How was I supposed to learn?"

Reese had grown up a rich kid in Los Angeles with chefs and cleaning people—Elena wasn't exactly sure about the extent of their domestic help. Despite the obvious differences in their backgrounds, Elena got lucky in the roommate lottery. Reese had become one of her closest friends in the two months since they'd started their freshman year at Dawson University.

"Fine, you made your point." Elena might joke about Reese not lifting a finger in the kitchen, but she secretly didn't mind cooking. Much like creating solutions in her chemistry labs, fussing around with food and experimenting with spices calmed her. Only today's lab hadn't calmed her. It had turned her into a frazzled mess. "I'm kind of busy, Reese. What's up?"

Reese stared at her shiny, cobalt-painted nails. "Oh, nothing. Just that you might want to toss in laundry duty along with meal prep after what I've arranged."

"Don't get your hopes up." Elena quit the online map and rifled through her backpack for the piece of paper she'd scribbled her professor's email address on. She hated going to one of the professors, but who else could get her inside a chemistry lab? "I'm in a rush, Reese. Tell me what it is already."

Her roommate rose quickly from the bed, excitement pouring off her as she paced the room. "Let's just say if everything works out, we won't have any problem getting into bars."

"Bars? You're thinking about…" Elena shook her head. "It doesn't matter. I have no interest in going to bars. And anyway, we're underage. There's no way the bouncers would let us in."

"They will if we have IDs that say we're twenty-one. You said you didn't like partying at the fraternity houses. This solves the problem."

Elena closed her eyes. She loved Reese, she really did, but sometimes they might as well be from different planets for how alike they were. "I'm not even going to ask how you managed to get us fake IDs."

Reese winked and walked toward the door.

"Wait," Elena called out. "Before you go, can you help me with something? I need a lab. One that's open after classes. I…screwed up an experiment today. I have to work it out before the exam or my grade will take a beating." Which was partially true. Elena was on scholarship; grades mattered. But mostly she needed to make sure she wasn't losing her ever-lovin' mind.

Liquids boiling without heat? Not possible. Yet it had happened. Twice.

Reese had crafty ways of getting what she needed on campus— case in point, the fake IDs—and it often involved something not altogether legal. But Elena was past caring about stuff like that. This was an emergency.

Reese rested her hand on the doorknob. "Try our neighbor. He's a chem geek like you, only way better looking than the students you hang out with."

Elena rolled her eyes. She and her chemistry friends might be geeks, but Reese was one of the biggest geeks—just in a pretty, less socially awkward package. She was a double major in political science and philosophy. Elena had learned the first week of school to never debate with Reese unless she wanted her ass handed to her.

"He seems connected in the department," Reese continued. "He could be a good resource."

"How do you even know these things?"

She blinked innocently. "Did you not hear my reference to his hotness? Need I say more?"

Elena closed her eyes and gave her head a shake. "No. No, you don't."

Even if the only reason her roommate knew about this guy was because she'd scouted out all the attractive coeds by major and place of residence, this was a good lead. The best Elena had that didn't involve speaking to a professor. She preferred begging their neighbor to help her find a lab over hiding the truth from someone who could get her kicked out of the chemistry department.

What person made liquids boil by waving their hands? No one, that's who. Which was why she needed to find the scientific cause.

Elena slid on her leather bomber. The jacket had been her late father's, and now she wore it, along with the amethyst necklace her mother had left behind. Her parents had been gone a long time, but holding on to their things made her feel less alone. If ever there was a time she needed a piece of them near, it was now.

"Don't come home too late," Reese said. "You just turned eighteen; we have cake to devour. I queued up *She's All That* on Netflix. And if I can convince you to go, there's a party on A Street. We need to celebrate."

Elena had almost forgotten it was her birthday. She'd woken not feeling well, and the day had deteriorated from there.

Reese didn't say the party was at a fraternity, but most of the parties she went to were. If Elena had wanted to hang out in a place that smelled like men's gym socks and stale beer, she could have invited her cousin Mateo to stay for a few days. No offense to the fraternity party, but a calm night with trashy food and a nineties movie worked.

She grabbed her backpack and followed her roommate out. "Cake and a movie sounds perfect. I'll see you a little later."

With any luck, her neighbor could help her gain access to a lab and she'd find a reasonable explanation for why crap was boiling. She prayed it was that simple.

But life had never been simple.

Elena rapped twice at the house next door. Her street was a mix of off-campus dorms, like the one she and Reese lived in, and regular student housing.

After a moment, the door opened, and the sharp scent of pot smoke billowed out. A boy with a long knobbed nose, whose head came to her shoulders, stood on the other side.

He leaned against the doorjamb and raked his gaze down her body.

Elena groaned internally. Most bizarre thing ever. At five foot ten, she never failed to attract guys she towered over. But she'd stopped trying to figure out the opposite sex ages ago. Her boyfriends were her beaker and the periodic table—two things in life that never failed her.

Well, until they had. That's why she was standing on her stoner neighbor's doorstep. Her beaker boyfriend had just dropped her on her ass.

"Which one of you is a chem major?" *Wow, smooth. Simmer down already and show some social skills.* She cleared her throat and tried again. "Sorry, I'm Elena, your neighbor. I heard one of you studies chemistry. I could use some advice."

Okay, not advice, per se, but no need to get into the dirty details until she was talking to the right person.

The guy in front of her banged a fist against an interior wall. "Derek!" he yelled, and sauntered to the left.

Elena tentatively stepped inside. Another stoner sat on a couch in the living room, where the first boy had returned to, zoned out and with a psychedelic-swirled bong in his hand.

Excellent. So far, neither of these guys looked like they could hold a pencil, let alone measure the pH of an acid.

Footsteps thundered down the stairs and a third person emerged, causing Elena's stomach to hitch. This guy must be Derek. And yes, she got why Reese had noticed *him.* Elena was antisocial, not dead.

Reese was right. Derek wasn't like the other students in her department. His clothes were normal, if a bit baggy, and his golden-brown hair was a rumpled mess, as if he'd risen from his bed and hadn't even bothered to run his fingers through it. But with a square jawline, heavy brow, and sensual lips, he was rather intimidating in the holy-hotness department. And tall.

Because Elena was the height of an average man, taller men turned her head. If she was paying attention.

Derek took in her face, his eyes widening. For a moment, it seemed as though he recognized her, which was odd, because he didn't look familiar. He peered down on her from a good half a foot, but she would have noticed him even if he didn't have the height to make her insides gooey. Derek lived in the house next door—an entire lawn away. And that might explain why she'd never seen him before. Elena was observant in class, not so much with her fellow students.

"You're a chemistry major?" she asked.

He blinked but otherwise made no response.

Okayyy. She took that to mean yes.

She glanced at the two characters on the couch, their eyes

rimmed with red, glassy, and half-lidded. They weren't paying attention, but she wanted privacy. "Can we talk somewhere?"

Derek led her to a dingy kitchen and turned a mismatched chair around. He slumped into it, facing her, and draped one long arm across the dining table. His hand was as big as her foot, and she wore size eights. He wasn't overtly muscled like the athletes at Dawson, but his broad back and shoulders stood out beneath the oversized T-shirt he wore. In some ways he was like a puppy—all limbs and paws—but he carried himself well for such a tall guy.

And why was she focusing on the way this guy looked? She had important things to worry about.

She sat in the seat beside him and smoothed back her wavy hair before reciting the speech she'd prepared on her way over. "My name's Elena. I live in the complex next door. I'm a chemistry major too." In a moment of inspiration, she flashed the Rosales smile her cousin Mateo claimed opened doors.

Derek's hand flexed, but his face remained unmoved.

Gahh. Why did she think she could charm this guy? She'd never had Mateo's ability with people.

She sat up and came straight to the point. "I was wondering if you know of any campus labs available for private use."

"Private use?" They were the first words Derek had uttered, and they delivered the same punch to her gut as his entrance in the hallway.

Elena shifted in her seat. The low, warm tone of his voice or the fact that she was asking for something highly unethical—probably both—sent prickles across her shoulders.

His gaze narrowed, and he took more than a cursory glance at her face this time, his look delving, as if he could see inside her head to the secrets she hid.

"My class labs aren't open after hours," she hurried on, "but tonight I have to practice." She nervously rubbed her thigh with the heel of her hand, freezing when his eyes caught the motion.

"Practice." His tone mocked.

Okay, he was right not to believe her, but still. "Yes. Practice."

This wasn't going well. Arrogant men drove her nuts, and there was something inherently superior about Derek's demeanor. Her frustration rose, and he hadn't even said yes or no yet. She mentally counted to five...

The liquids shouldn't have boiled. There had to be a reason, and she'd figure it out with or without this guy's help.

Should she leave?

Elena shoved a dark curl from her face and huffed out a breath. Derek's assessing stare rose from her eyes to the curl—and lingered.

Was he passing some sort of judgment based on her looks? And okay, maybe she'd just done the same to him. Elena was lighter due to her mother's coloring, or so she'd been told—she'd never known her mom. But even with half of her mother's genes, she looked Mexican with her big, wavy hair, according to the white people in her hometown. Could Derek tell what she was? Did he have something against it?

Discrimination back home was subtle—little things like shop owners being less welcoming to her and her aunt compared to how they greeted white customers. Elena had learned to ignore it, but in this instance, the judgement rankled.

"Forget it." She stood and reached for her backpack. She might be jumping to conclusions about the prejudice thing, but it was obvious Derek wasn't going to help her.

"Stop." Though he'd spoken softly, his voice commanded.

Normally a tone like that would have ticked her off, but for some reason Elena eased back into the seat.

"I know of a place," he said carefully. "My mentor's...out of town. You can use his lab."

Seriously? She'd hoped for this, but she hadn't actually believed an undergrad would have access to a private lab.

Before she could second-guess his motives or consider all the reasons why this was a bad idea, she said, "Thank you."

Derek tapped his finger on the table, his dark blue eyes studying her again.

Her heartbeat spiked, and she broke eye contact. She wasn't used to attractive guys staring at her, unless they were five foot four and fantasized about dating an Amazon. "So can I go there now? Do I need a key?"

Derek stood, pulled out a cell phone from his pocket, and glanced at the screen. "Give me five minutes. I'll walk you over."

He's going too?

She jumped up and jerked on her backpack, accidentally knocking into Derek's arm. With her chest.

Not the first time her boobs had collided with an unsuspecting object, just the most embarrassing.

Elena froze then carefully eased back an inch, only to find that the air between them had changed the way it did before a lightning storm—positive and negative molecules separating, creating the urgency to rush back together. She glared at the empty space between them, as if it, like the liquid anomalies, had betrayed her.

Slowly, she scanned up Derek's broad chest and shoulders, beyond the firm jaw, tangling momentarily with his full lips, and landing on his eyes. He was staring down, his beautiful gaze almost threatening, as though he sensed the crackling and blamed it on *her*.

And maybe it was her fault. She didn't know what came from her and what didn't. Or why strange things kept happening today.

"You don't have to go with me," she said. "I can find it. There's no need to put you out."

Of course he'd *want* to go. It was his lab. But she didn't need a witness. Bad enough her classmates had been around for the incident this afternoon. She'd cleaned it up quickly without anyone noticing, but privacy, a safe place to figure things out—that was what she needed.

Derek's jaw hardened. "Either I go with you or you can forget about the lab."

She didn't like his tone, but how many people had access to a private lab? It was a strange coincidence her neighbor happened to, but Elena wasn't going to question her good fortune.

Maybe she should have.

Chapter 2

Derek's heavy tread on the pebbled path fell silent as he turned up a campus sidewalk and loped up concrete steps to a two-story beige building with steel overhangs. Elena had seen the building before, but she'd never been inside. From what she understood, it housed upper-division professors' offices.

She followed Derek up the steps, and he held the door for her. As soon as she entered the building, he passed her in two long strides and jogged up a flight of stairs.

The air on the second level smelled of formaldehyde and cleaning products, leaving a bitter taste on her tongue. Some of the doors were labeled with professors' names, while others were numbered laboratories. Derek stopped at the last lab on the right, and Elena's grip on the padded straps of her backpack tightened.

Her hands had been trembling all day. This morning she'd assumed she drank too much caffeine, but her last double latte had been hours ago, and still the shaking continued.

Derek opened the door to the lab and flipped on light switches.

Elena's breath caught. For a moment, she forgot everything—her trembling hands, the liquid crisis...

She stepped inside and spun slowly around. Aside from an odd section of antique devices and bottles—*was that a vintage Bunsen burner?*—every piece of cool chem equipment she'd ever dreamed of using stood in front of her. Some were so high-tech even her class labs didn't carry them.

Derek's gaze narrowed on her face, and his lips compressed.

So maybe she'd been grinning from ear to ear. Who wouldn't be in the mecca of all labs?

Refocusing, she set her backpack on one of two work islands. "Any special rules you want me to follow?" If she couldn't figure out a solution to her problem with access to this equipment, she never would.

"Yeah. Don't use anything you've never used before. And don't blow anything up."

Haha, funny—if it wasn't actually a risk. But he didn't know that. "I'm not an amateur."

His sculpted eyebrow rose. "Aren't you? Isn't that why you wanted to *practice*?"

He wouldn't believe her if she told him about class and the water at home. She had no one to confide in. Reese had become her closest friend since starting Dawson, but their friendship was new. Elena wasn't ready to share this with her, let alone a guy she hardly knew.

She ignored the question and let out a slow breath. *Act normal.* "Who else uses this place besides you and your mentor?"

"No one."

"You have it all to yourself?" She peered around. The lab was large enough to support several scientists. "How'd you get so lucky?"

Derek unloaded books from his backpack onto a desk in the corner. "I published in a major medical journal in high school."

Elena chuckled, then noticed his serious expression.

Holy crap. Only kid wonders published in scientific journals. The rest of the authors were seasoned experts. "So you're, what, some kind of genius?"

"I'm not a genius. My memory is—" He stacked the last book on his desk. "Advanced," he finally said.

"What do you mean *advanced*? Are we talking photographic?"

He shrugged. "Something like that. I took extra classes during high school at the nearby university. My dad's a cardiologist. With his help, I researched proteomics and immunization. Professor St. Just, who's now my mentor, heard about my project and asked me to work with him at Dawson."

Most high school students weren't far enough along in school to take college courses. Even so, the chemistry class Elena had taken at the junior college near her podunk farm town was nothing compared to what this guy had done. His accomplishments made her look average.

"If that's the case, why did you choose Dawson? Why not attend Harvard or Johns Hopkins?" Not that she was putting down Dawson. It was a top university. But there were *top* schools and then there were *elite* schools.

He shrugged, tucking his backpack beneath the desk. "Marlon —Professor St. Just—offered something those programs couldn't."

"A sports car?"

His gaze slid to her. "Funny." No hint of mirth crossed his handsome face. "He offered exclusive anytime access to his lab."

"I would've taken the car," she said, though it wasn't true. She would have taken the lab as well because it was kick-ass. But for some reason, she needed to ruffle this guy's steely exterior.

Derek's mouth twitched. "Don't make me regret bringing you here."

Grumpy with no sense of humor. But beggars couldn't be choosers and all that. She needed his lab. For her sanity, if nothing else. Still… "Why did you bring me?"

He shrugged and paced to a locker. He pulled out a lab coat and other protective equipment. "You seemed desperate."

She hadn't said anything to that effect, which meant he'd read her without words. And that was unsettling.

She didn't want this guy reading her and discovering the truth.

Stupid, Derek thought. Why *had* he brought Elena? Because she'd seemed desperate? Partly true. He wasn't sure about the complete answer, didn't want to think that deeply. All he knew was that the minute they stepped into Marlon's lab, he wanted to take it back. Tell her she shouldn't be there, that he couldn't help her. He couldn't risk ruining what he'd built with Marlon, and he'd had his reasoning rock-solid in the kitchen, totally prepared to say no. Then she'd smiled.

Blinded by a pretty girl.

Derek wasn't normal under any circumstances—why he'd gone and done the most stereotypical guy thing and given in to a pretty girl's smile, he hadn't a clue. It was annoying as hell.

Elena didn't explain outright why she wanted the lab, but she wore her fiery emotions like a neon sign. He could tell she wasn't giving him the whole truth. He couldn't decide whether getting involved had been smart or stupid, but he was leaning toward stupid.

Derek couldn't risk distractions from his work. Not if he wanted control over his life.

He pulled out his notebook, attempting to relax. So far, Elena had done things correctly. Worn the proper safety equipment, laid out her tools in the order in which she'd use them, and retrieved chemicals he deemed safe for a rudimentary chemist. She was pretty methodical about the whole thing, which surprised him. Maybe he hadn't watched his neighbor closely enough. She knew her way around a lab better than he'd expected.

Tapping his finger, he stared at her hands. He couldn't be sure from this distance, but he thought they might be trembling. If they were, that wasn't a good sign. Measuring chemicals requires a steady hand for precision. Still, she seemed competent enough, and more important, the chemicals she had before her were harmless.

Long, dark lashes shadowed the smooth skin on her cheeks as she focused on the flask over the burner... This was totally distracting. He needed to stop staring.

Elena didn't realize it, but he knew who she was, had noticed her months ago. Not that he had any intention of telling her that.

He attempted to study his notebook, but his attention, if not his gaze, was still on his neighbor. From his periphery, he saw her glance up and turn her back to him. He peered over. Was she waving her hands?

The flask in front of her rattled, and Elena lurched back. The solution hissed and spurted, shooting everywhere—including onto her—right before the container holding it crashed onto the floor, piercing the room with the sound of shattering glass.

Derek's heart stopped, then pumped double-time as he careened across the room, knocking over a stool.

Elena pressed her hands to her face, her eyes wide. The strange liquid glowed fluorescent across her lightly tanned skin, dripping down her chin.

He yanked off her lab coat and pushed her toward the emergency shower.

She followed him blindly for a moment, then pulled back, wiping the solution off her face with her sleeve. "I'm fine. I just used too much heat. I'll clean up the mess right away."

He stared in disbelief. "What are you talking about? That stuff's all over you. We're taking decontamination measures." He wasn't sure how she'd managed an explosion with the materials in front of her, but he wasn't taking chances.

"It's not necessary. I wasn't using anything dangerous." She tried to walk past him, and swayed as though she was lightheaded.

Derek caught her by the shoulders. He studied her face and the skin of her neck. Whatever that fluorescent crap was, it had scorched her flesh a light shade of pink. "You're taking a cold shower."

"No. I don't need it." Her tone came out adamant, but her body shook.

Chemical accidents were nothing to mess with. She could be in shock, and he didn't trust her to make sound decisions right now. She attempted to duck around him again, but he reached under her knees and swept her into his arms. She weighed nothing. But with his unusual strength, everything weighed nothing.

Elena glanced around, her eyes widening. "What are you doing? Put me down!"

He set her beneath the shower and turned on the nozzle before she could wiggle her way out. Water drenched her hair and clothes in seconds. She sucked in a startled breath.

If Elena couldn't think clearly right now, he needed to. "Take them off." He gestured to the long-sleeved shirt and jeans she wore.

Water poured down her face, her eyelids fluttering beneath the onslaught. "*No way.* You're being ridiculous. I told you, the chemicals were harmless."

He sighed in frustration. "The chemicals you started with were harmless, not the fluorescent stuff that ended up all over you. I don't even know what that shit was. This is for your safety; we don't have time for modesty. Take them off."

Her body trembled and her teeth chattered—the water pouring over her was cold. Her eyes darted to the side as though she were considering what he'd said. "I was wearing a lab coat. No —nothing got on my clothes. Only a little on my skin where the coat didn't cover. I could have flushed my face beneath the faucet."

She had a point. "At least remove your shirt. That solution was dripping down your neck."

Elena huffed out a sigh of annoyance, then reached down and whipped off her top.

It landed with a splat on the shower floor. Or at least, he thought it did. He wasn't looking at the piece of fabric on the ground.

This was bad. Worse than he could have imagined.

Her skin was fine. No scorch marks below her neck, just like she'd said, but he could see everything down to her toned stomach.

Beautiful didn't begin to describe Elena. She was...more.

Derek's mouth went dry. He tried not to look at her curves

beneath the pale lace bra that had become transparent with water, but—yeah, that was impossible.

She shivered as she rinsed her face and hair, her technique choppy and not nearly thorough enough. "Happy?"

"No." He kept his eyes above her neck and shoved up the sleeves of his shirt. "Hold still."

He traced her cheekbones with the tips of his fingers, making circular motions over her face, careful to reach the places she'd missed. He rubbed her stubborn chin and down her long, delicate neck, moving the necklace she wore aside to reach her skin. Working his way farther south, his hands stilled above the slopes of her breasts.

Sweat beaded on his temples, the room suddenly burning hot despite the cold water that was still running. Derek dabbed his forehead with the sleeve on his upper arm and looked at her face. Big mistake.

Liquid hazel depths stared back, the pupils dilated to half the iris.

Elena slapped his hands away. "We're good. You got it all."

He stepped back and thrust wet fists into the front pockets of his jeans. He had to get a grip. She had caused a damned explosion in Marlon's lab. He needed to distance himself from her, not feel things for her.

She turned off the water and swayed as she bent down for her shirt.

Derek's jaw clenched. He went to steady her again, but she stepped around him and wrung out the fabric. "I'm fine, just cold."

She didn't look fine. The scorch marks had gone away—surprisingly fast, actually—but she looked pale and ready to pass out.

He peeled off the long-sleeved shirt he'd worn over his tee and handed it to her.

"Thanks." She slipped it on, and the material draped her like a dress.

Wrapping her arms around her waist, she turned and walked toward her work area, her legs moving stiffly in the damp jeans.

"What are you doing?"

"Cleaning up," she said without looking back.

"Do *not* take another step. Matter of fact, grab your things and walk out the door. You're done."

Elena's back tensed. She looked over her shoulder, blinking several times. "It was an accident. It won't happen again."

"You're right, it won't," he bit out. "I need this lab. I should never have brought you here."

Elena couldn't have caused an explosion with the materials she'd been using, and yet somehow she had. She was trouble, and she wasn't coming anywhere near his lab again. He had enough to worry about with his mentor missing. "Leave. Now."

A flare of fire turned her hazel eyes deep emerald. She stormed to the locker, grabbed her things, and slammed the door shut. When it didn't catch, she slammed it again.

Why was she so pissed? He was the one with the contamination zone to clean up. "Wait outside. I'll walk you home when I'm finished."

Elena grabbed her folder from the island, water trickling off her jeans in a wet trail as she swept out the door without slowing.

Of course she wouldn't wait.

He assessed the mess and rubbed his forehead. If Marlon suddenly showed up and walked in on this, he'd be pissed, but Derek couldn't let Elena walk home by herself in the dark. He'd become paranoid since his eighteenth birthday. He didn't take chances.

He strode out of the room and spotted her at the end of the hallway. She shot him an icy glare he interpreted as *Stay the hell away.*

Change of plans. He'd follow her to make sure she got home safely, but she wouldn't know he was there.

No one saw him once he Blended.

Chapter 3

Elena stared at the PowerPoint slide on the large screen in the physics auditorium. What the hell was going on? She didn't need her reading glasses today—a first for her. But it wasn't just her eyes. The percussion of hundreds of fingers flying over keyboards as students took notes sounded like a million tiny mice scampering across a wooden floor, each key pounding into her skull.

This morning, she'd hoped things would be back to normal, that yesterday would be some weird dream she'd wake from. But the liquids *were* real, her hands still shook, and now her senses were in hyper mode.

She hunched in her seat and winced. After gaining access to the most amazing chem lab she'd ever seen last night, she was no closer to explaining how she made the liquids boil. She didn't dare experiment at home after the mess she'd created in front of Derek. Which had been followed by one of the most embarrassing shower scenes ever.

Elena had been so shocked by the explosion she'd lost all sense of safety. Derek was right to throw her in the shower. Harmless chemicals or not, they hadn't reacted as expected. But when he helped her remove the solution, she wasn't thinking about the danger of the chemicals on her body. She was too busy being stunned by the effect his *touch* had on her.

Her attraction to him should have been the last thing on her mind, but her breath had quickened and her heart raced in her chest. She was sure he could tell what he was doing to her.

It was no surprise Derek told her to leave. He'd been a bit of a jerk about it, but she couldn't blame him for getting her out of there. Overnight, she'd gone from a budding chemist at the top of her class to a menace with lab equipment. Everything she knew about science was dissolving. If she could accidentally boil her solution, what else could she accidentally boil?

Jesus—people were roughly sixty percent water. What if she boiled the liquids inside herself? *Or inside someone else?*

She had to figure this out before something terrible happened.

Elena breathed deeply, attempting to calm down, but it wasn't working. Because as soon as she returned her attention to the professor, her heightened senses zeroed in on a door behind the podium that was the same color as the wall.

A door she'd never seen before.

Maybe it had been there all along. She could just be searching for things because she'd become an overanxious crazy person these last twenty-four hours.

The door swung open.

Dammit. And if that wasn't enough to convince her the door was strange, another classroom lay beyond. A classroom that shouldn't exist because it was physically impossible. Her physics auditorium filled the entire first floor of the building.

Elena stared into the other room. Everything in there appeared larger: the people, the ornate desks spread farther apart than the stadium seating of her auditorium. It was like looking through a magnifying glass. What the hell?

She wrapped her arms around her chest and clenched her elbows. Right now, sprawling farms and the single stoplight of her California hometown sounded nice.

A tall blond guy in dark, fitted clothes sitting near the door in the strange classroom turned and looked right at her, a slow, knowing smile spreading across his face.

Her back tensed. Why was he looking at her like that?

Before she could consider it further, he rose and strolled out of sight, giving her a clear view of the rest of the students. A few of them had light brown hair, but most were blondes or redheads with smooth, pale skin. All of them were unnaturally attractive like the first guy, who could have been a Viking warrior with his height and broad shoulders.

Dawson University was known for its diversity. This Norse group looked out of place.

Elena glared at her physics professor, but the woman didn't seem aware of the room behind her.

She nudged the girl next to her, who was texting. "Do you see that?"

The girl's gaze went straight to the professor, as though the other room wasn't important—or not there. Her long, side-swept bangs dropped over one eye. "See what?"

Elena opened her mouth to say something, then shook her head. "Nothing, I—did they paint the wall a different color? Wasn't it maroon?"

Her neighbor edged to the far side of her seat. The girl's body was angled away, but the screen of her phone was visible. She texted, *Freak next to me in Phys 4.*

Great. A quick scan confirmed the rest of the auditorium wasn't looking at the strangers in the other room either. Their attentions were focused on the PowerPoint images overhead, even though the room stuck out like Elena's wavy hair on a humid day.

Rubbing her temples, she faced forward—and her heart launched into her throat.

The strangers beyond the wall had gathered into a semicircle. And they were all watching her.

The physics professor clicked off her laser pointer and crossed the podium, showing zero signs that she noticed the people inches away. She flipped on the auditorium's bright lights. Lecture over.

Students emptied desks—Elena's neighbor like a fire had been lit beneath her butt. The crowd blocked Elena's view of the podium and wall for several minutes.

By the time the last person moved out of the way, the door to the other classroom had closed, all evidence of the strangers gone.

Elena shoved her laptop into her backpack and swung the bag over her shoulder. She strode to the front of the classroom. The professor was busy talking to students and didn't seem to notice her. She hesitated for only a moment before reaching for the indentation of the hidden door.

The surface was smooth, no grooves, but she could still see the edges. How was that possible?

She peered from various angles and continued to feel around the wall, pressing in different places. That was when she saw the faint outline of a doorknob the same color as the wall halfway down.

Elena reached for the knob. And her fingers slipped straight through as if it were air, her knuckles bumping the wall instead.

She stepped back, shaking her head. The door had opened. It was real. She'd prove it.

She ran out of the auditorium toward the end of the building where the other classroom should be.

And came to a dead end.

No doors. No creases in the wall. Nothing to indicate anything lay beyond.

Elena kicked the surface hard with the tip of her sneaker, the impact reverberating up her leg. The wall was solid.

Why was this happening? She sank to the ground and pressed her fingers to her eyelids. She tried to concentrate on what she knew—to piece it together and make sense of it all.

Logically, the room couldn't exist. She'd walked past the Physics Hall every day for the last two months. No buildings backed the structure, not even a temp, but the door and the class-room—the students—she'd *seen* them.

Last night, she'd humiliated herself in front of Derek, could have injured both of them. Nothing should have happened with the chemicals she'd been using, but it had. And now her hearing was elevated and she was seeing things she couldn't explain?

She needed to see a doctor, because something was seriously wrong.

Nothing in life had come easily. Her mother had left her and her father on Elena's first birthday, and then the universe took away her father a few short years later. Those were things she couldn't control and had never understood. But school made sense—science and chemistry, molecules and the predictable ways they reacted. She trusted it to be there for her.

Now her foothold in life was failing her too.

Her head pounding, Elena lumbered to her feet and started to run, her backpack slapping her spine, threatening to unbalance her.

She rounded a corner, desperate for an exit—and slammed into a large body. Air burst from her lungs, stars flittering across her vision. And then the giant wall of a human she'd bounced into grabbed her and picked her up.

"I wondered where you had gone." The unfamiliar, melodic voice rumbled through the chest her face was plastered against.

Elena couldn't breathe and her arms were pinned. The man began to move, carrying her away.

She angled her mouth past the thick fabric of his shirt and sucked in air. "Let me go. Help!" she yelled, but his grip tightened and the slight view she had revealed the hallways were empty.

Her struggles grew frantic and she kicked her legs to free herself. The man shifted her body to the side, and that was when she saw his face.

The Viking with the wry smile.

She hadn't imagined him...and now he was abducting her?

Elena's blood whooshed through her veins, the throbbing increasing the headache her heightened senses had triggered.

Before she could figure out how to get away, the Viking opened a door and unceremoniously dropped her on her feet.

She spun around, ready to dart in the opposite direction, and froze. Ornate desks, intricate plasterwork—it was the classroom that shouldn't exist.

Three adults sat behind a wide table like magistrates. A woman with silver, wavy hair and piercing blue eyes nodded to the Viking. "Thank you, Keen." She regarded Elena. "Good morning."

Elena glanced behind her to find her kidnapper blocking the exit. "What's this about? Where am I?"

The woman's smile was cold. "In due time. For now, all that matters is that we know about you, Elena Rosales."

Elena had never seen these people in her life. "What do you mean, you know me?"

A man and another woman sat there too. The man had a spray of gray at his temples and the other woman had short red hair, but all three of them had smooth, creamy skin. They wore fitted, dark clothing, like the Viking who'd grabbed her, and were slender and unusually tall, even while seated.

It was the first time Elena had ever felt like the short person in the room.

"We know who your mother is, why you were recruited by Dawson, and what you've done."

Elena had received a full-ride scholarship. It was more than she'd ever hoped for... Had that been intentional? "Wait—" She shook her head. "How do you know my mother? I don't even know my mother."

The woman smiled that cold smile again. "No, you wouldn't."

That's all she was going to say? No explanation?

"You've been using your magic." This time the comment came from the man. His features were Nordic, like those of her captor, but sharper, more chiseled, with a longer nose and high cheekbones.

Elena's brain blew a fuse at his words. A long pause followed while she wrapped her head around it. "My *magic*?" The prickles along her skin returned full force. "I'm sorry—" She gestured to him.

"Leo."

"—Leo. If you're referring to the lab—ah, labs—that was an accident. Won't happen again." *She hoped.*

Leo exchanged a look with the two women at his side.

"Oh, but we want it to happen again," the silver-haired woman said. "In fact, we count on it."

The red-haired lady with delicate features remained perfectly silent.

Elena fought a shiver. The liquid disasters, these people with their strange doors and knowledge about her missing mother—there was something very, very wrong with this situation. Still, given the size of Keen behind her and how easily he'd deposited her here, she chose her next words cautiously. "I don't know what happened in the labs."

"Don't you?" the older woman asked. "I think you know exactly what you did, Elena Rosales."

The solutions had exploded, but there was something—something she'd ignored yesterday because it was insanity. Before the explosions, the shaking and tingling in her fingers had magnified...as if an energy simmered beneath her skin.

This was nuts.

The woman nodded. "I see from your expression that you agree."

Elena's control slipped, panic tightening her chest. "Who are you?" she choked out, glancing around the room more thoroughly.

A large map with odd land formations hung behind them, and there was state-of-the-art computer equipment below wavy-paned diamond glass windows. The contrast of old and new reminded her of Derek's lab and the antique equipment next to modern devices.

"You've already been introduced to Leo," the silver-haired woman said. "I am Portia, and this is Deirdre." She gestured to the silent redhead. Portia pursed her lips as though she'd tasted something sour. "They said you were bright for a human, but you are proving particularly dense."

"For a *human?*"

Portia waved her hand to Keen and the others at the table. "We are Fae. And you are Halven—half Fae from your mother's side."

Grab *Fates Divided* Now!

BOOKS BY JULES BARNARD

HALVEN RISING SERIES

Fates Altered (Prequel)

Fates Divided (Book 1)

Fates Entwined (Book 2)

Fates Fulfilled (Book 3)

Complete book catalog available at:

WWW.JULESBARNARD.COM

ABOUT THE AUTHOR

Jules Barnard is a *USA Today* bestselling author of contemporary romance and romantic fantasy. Her contemporary series include the Never Date and Cade Brothers series. She also writes romantic fantasy under the same pen name in the Halven Rising series *Library Journal* calls "…an exciting new fantasy adventure." Regardless of genre, Jules spins addictive stories filled with heart and humor.

When Jules isn't in her sweatpants writing and rewarding herself with chocolate, she spends her time with her husband and two children in their small hometown on the Pacific Coast. She credits herself with the ability to read while running on the treadmill or burning dinner.

**To learn more about Jules, visit her website:
https://julesbarnard.com/**

You can also sign up for Jules's newsletter, and receive writing updates:
julesbarnard.com/newsletterparanormal/

Or consider following Jules on Instagram:
www.instagram.com/julesbarnardauthor **and**
www.instagram.com/halvenrisingseries

Made in the USA
Monee, IL
22 June 2021